M   Bagby, George. *33,232*
     The most wanted.

THE MOST WANTED

George Bagby

THE
MOST
WANTED

Published for the Crime Club
by
Doubleday & Company, Inc.
Garden City, New York
1983

All of the characters in this book are fictitious,
and any resemblance to actual persons,
living or dead,
is purely coincidental.

Library of Congress Cataloging in Publication Data

Bagby, George, 1906–
The Most Wanted.
I. Title.
PS3537.T3184M6   1983   813'.52
ISBN 0-385-18925-7

Library of Congress Catalog Card Number 83-45015
Copyright © 1983 by Doubleday & Company, Inc.
All Rights Reserved
Printed in the United States of America

First Edition

To

the memory of James Sandoe,
scholar, wit, critic, and friend.

THE MOST WANTED

CHAPTER 1

Of the people who had known Lansing Monroe I suppose only his murderer knew of his death before I got the word. I have something like an inside track. Although I, George Bagby, am a writer and have no official connection with the police, I come as close to being a part of Homicide, NYPD, as any outsider could be. The Chief of Homicide is Inspector Schmidt, and Schmitty has long been my friend. It began as a business arrangement with me writing the accounts of the inspector's investigations.

Early on, however, Schmitty took to keeping me around throughout the hunt, following his every physical move even when I might need some assistance in following his mental processes. For long periods of time, therefore, we are together in shared experience and shared hazard. Two men can hardly sustain such a relationship unless they are friends.

Departmental routine brings immediate report of all murders to the inspector. Whenever something comes along that shows any potential of being good copy, Schmitty gives me the quick word. Although the Lansing Monroe killing at first sight showed no such promise, he, nevertheless, gave me a ring.

"I've got one here," he said. "It's nothing at all. Looks like a gang job. So it's the airtight cover-up. Maybe we'll crack it and maybe we won't. Which is going to depend on whether or not we can get our hands on someone who'll sing. You know what that's like—just dull, slogging routine."

"You've had a couple of those develop into good stories," I said.

I was thinking that he would have liked to have me in but was warning me of possible boredom.

"Only after someone began talking," he said. "If we get that lucky on this one and the tune sounds good, that will be plenty of time for you to start on it. The only reason I'm calling you is I think maybe you'd want to hear. It could be a guy you know, but if it is that one, it seems to me it was nobody you liked much."

"Who?"

"The name rang a bell and I couldn't think what. Then it seemed like you mentioned the name a couple of times. Does Lansing Monroe mean anything to you?"

I almost laughed. "The name," I said. "The name, yes; but a gang killing? That has to be some other Lansing Monroe. It can't be the guy I know."

"Come on, kid. We're not talking John Smiths. There can't be many Lansing Monroes."

"Okay," I said. "If it's the one I know, then it can't be a gang killing."

"Hey, Baggy. You going snob on me all of a sudden?"

"My Lansing Monroe is a twerp. No gang would ever bother about him, much less think he was worth bumping."

"Well-nourished Caucasian male." The inspector was reading from the report that had been bucked through to him. "Six foot one; 185 pounds; gray eyes; brown hair—red dyed but showing brown and gray near the scalp. Your guy?"

"I was going to say it could be, but the hair dye is the clincher. Last time I saw him he had it. He was taking a lot of riding about it."

"There's also an appendectomy scar," Schmitty said, "but you wouldn't know about that."

"I do know. That checks too."

"You know?"

"Club locker room. He did a lot of walking around naked. He kept in great shape. He liked displaying his flat belly and inviting people to punch it hard."

"So somebody's punched it full of holes," the inspector said. "He was machine-gunned, mowed down during the night in Riverside Park, stitched straight across the belly."

"He was a twerp, but for twerpitude," I said, "that was excessive."

"For what?"

"Twerpitude."

"Is that a word?"

"It is now. I just made it up."

"If you have to make words up, make up some easy ones. It wasn't for twerpitude."

"For what then?"

"One or another of the usual gang reasons. Maybe we'll find out."

"Anything you want from me?"

"If you think you know something that might help."

"I can't think of a thing. I hardly knew the guy apart from seeing him around the club. He always came on super-friendly, but that was just the way he was. We never were friends."

"Yeah, but if anything comes to you, let me know. It's likely he had a side to his life he kept thoroughly covered up. He maybe uncovered everything else in the club locker room, but probably not that."

CHAPTER 2

I try to think why I went to the funeral. He'd been a fellow-member of the club, and I'd seen a lot of him there. That might have made it seem the correct thing to do. We had never been close. I thought of him as a long-time acquaintance but never as a friend. I had the uncomfortable feeling, however, that for his part he had considered me a friend.

Now he was dead and death had come to him violently. I was bugged by the thought that death should have changed my attitude toward him. I couldn't feel right about there having been no change. I suppose in turning up at the funeral I had the notion that I was doing something I should have wanted to do. It wasn't as good as having all the right feelings, but it would at least be as much as I could manage.

According to the newspaper obituaries, he had no immediate family and was survived only by an uncle and a cousin—no widow, no children, no brothers, no sisters. That I learned it only from the papers is an indication of how little I knew the guy. It was the first I knew that he had never been married, and that was only a part of what I had never known. About even more casual acquaintances I know much more. I've seen pictures of the kiddies. I've known what the man did, not infrequently where he had gone to school.

That I'd known so little about Lansing Monroe could have been attributed to my lack of interest or even of curiosity. In consideration of the way he'd died, however, I was reassessing that. Perhaps I had known so little because he had wanted it that way. It could have been that he had been to that extent secretive.

So maybe that was my real reason for going to the funeral. For the first time I was curious about the man. Being there, however, only honed my curiosity to a sharper edge.

I expected something modest. When there is no immediate family to need the support of friends around them, people often feel no compunction about staying away. I thought there might be some business associates, if he had been in business. I didn't know even that much about him. There were also the guys at the club, particularly those of them who at one time or another had been accepting favors from him. He'd been a big one for doing favors.

As expected, a few of the men from the club did come. They bunched together and regarded everyone else with a curiosity that wasn't readily distinguishable from suspicion. The chief mourner was a great flabby hunk of old man in a wheelchair. He alternated great grief with greater irascibility. I was in no position to say that such unrestrained grief was unwarranted. I had no reason to doubt that he had been inordinately fond of his nephew. This would have to be the uncle.

In our culture, however, men, and with only the rare exception even women, suppress or at least tone down any public display of such extremes of emotion. The old man didn't go as far as gouging his cheeks with his fingernails, but his sobs were of seismic dimensions. His moans were stentorian. His invocations of God's pity were loud enough to reach the heavenly throne and beyond. His imprecations and calls for vengeance were not only thunderous but so bloodthirstily inventive that they could only have come from a man who was a dedicated old hand at calling down curses.

Ostensibly all of this was addressed to God, but I couldn't escape the impression that it was aimed rather more at us, the less-exalted audience gathered for the funeral service. I am inclined to say the same for the old man's outbursts of rage. They were targeted on a younger man who was pushing the wheelchair and hovering in attendance. Like the manifestations of grief and the calls for vengeance, they were geared to reach the larger audience.

The younger man looked to be of an age with Lansing Monroe. Early forties would have been a reasonable guess. He was performing the offices of a male nurse-companion, but he could never have been mistaken for one. He did the job with amateur clumsiness and under the old guy's abuse he showed a painful vulnerability. No hired companion would have held still for the half of it. The buckos that do that work are too much in demand. It's a sellers' market. It takes little to make them quit.

Settled as they were at the head of the aisle, the old man in addition to the sound of his voice was giving me a view of no more than the back of his head and some extensive edges of his bulk where they overflowed the wheelchair. His much-abused attendant, however, had to turn again and again to do some service for his tormentor. As soon as I'd had a good look at the younger man's face, I recognized him. On several occasions I'd seen him at the club with Monroe and, because of a strong resemblance, had assumed they were brothers. The obituaries, however, had said no brother. This then would be the cousin, either the old devil's son or another nephew.

Apart from the guys I knew, there were a few couples. They could have been friends or possibly relatives too distant to have been named among the survivors. The way they reacted to the old man's performance suggested that they were not family. They were all showing that inner struggle between astonished curiosity and a tactful effort to pretend there was nothing untoward happening.

On everyone else there I needed to make no guesses. If they weren't men I knew well, they were guys I knew by sight. Inspector Schmidt was there and, scattered about, a few of his Homicide boys. Those are all good friends. The buckos I knew only by sight might have been expected after what Schmitty had told me about Lansing Monroe's murder, except that I hadn't quite been able to believe him. As soon as I'd walked into the church, however, I'd known that I had to believe. Before I'd laid eyes on any of the assembled company I had seen the flowers. The published obituaries had requested that there be no flowers, suggesting that people contribute instead to their favorite charities.

But if a man is dead to all charity, surely this suggested alternative is no good to him. When gangsters send flowers, vast acreages are stripped of their blooms. Throughout the history of gangdom, flower shops have figured prominently as fronts for the illegal enterprises. Since the proprietors are to be their own best customers, it may well be that they like the idea of getting those great van loads of funeral pieces at wholesale.

Even if you've never had occasion to attend a gangster's funeral, you've heard about them. This was probably the first time that the services were held in one of Manhattan's more fashionable churches, but that was the only discernible difference. The flowers all but overflowed the place. Racked up behind the altar they hid from sight Stanford White's marble reredos. The famous architect, of course, had also been a murder victim. It may have been that they didn't want him getting into the act.

The presumptive donors were much in evidence—Smiley Donohue and Fats Jenkins. Each was accompanied by his standard retinue of bodyguards and henchmen. Those were all over the place, heavy-muscled, watchful men at the very peak of physical trim. Even if you didn't know the faces, you could tell them from Inspector Schmidt's plainclothes cops. They all wore those suits beautifully tailored to accommodate shoulder holster and weapon without showing more than the most barely perceptible bulge. Schmitty's boys are not so exquisitely tailored. On them the bulge of the .38 is visible even to the untutored eye.

Smiley Donohue—if you don't know, the name might suggest a jovial character. Nothing could be more amiss. Donohue has a facial scar, the mark of an old knife slash. It lifts the right side of his mouth in the travesty of a fixed grin. The left corner has never been known to lift. In left profile the mouth is unchangeably tight and mean.

In the case of Fats Jenkins there is no irony in the name. The man is monstrous. He's fat all over. In many respects his appearance fits the description in A Visit from St. Nicholas. He has the laugh and the belly that shakes like jelly, but there's never any twinkle in his eye. There's a vicious gleam.

I sat through the service wondering what the lads who'd known Monroe at the club and those polished, well-mannered couples could be thinking of the flowers and all that assembled muscle.

For me the pattern was too obvious. Lansing Monroe was having a gangster's funeral. One gang would be in attendance to pay respects to a fallen member. The other gang would have come to make a display of innocence. By their presence and their flowers they would be saying it was no work of theirs and reprisals should not be directed against them.

The service was as such services are when they are held over the body of a deceased who between his baptism and his funeral had never been to church. The minister held his part of it to the prescribed text. He made a valiant effort to come up with the name of the deceased without allowing it to be noticeable that he couldn't do it without consulting his notes. A friend, the male half of one of the couples, did the eulogy. He described Lansing Monroe much as Monroe had been wont to present himself—warm, friendly, generous, all those acts of kindness. If he had ever detected any suggestion of the bogus, he refrained from mentioning it.

The cousin spoke for the family. He went on at length about the good companion Lansing had been in their boyhood. With relish and humor he indicated that they had been companions in mischief. He looked as though he wished he hadn't brought that up when the old man interrupted from his wheelchair.

"That was you," the old devil said. "Lansing was always a good boy."

If there was to have been any further childhood reminiscences, the interruption cut them off. The talk shifted to a more recent date, to Lansing's "indefatigable kindness to my father, his uncle."

That got to be rather boring. I took to speculating on who was going to talk for the gangs. It was an entertaining speculation, but obviously they were no part of the official program.

After the service everybody stood in place while son wheeled father up the aisle to the tune of a non-stop critique of inept wheelchair technique. There was some good Bach going on the organ, but even with all the stops out the organ could have been no match to the roared imprecations.

Outside in the street the old man sat his wheelchair and people lined up to file past him and offer him and his son their condolences. Compared to the numbers that had been in the church the line was short. Smiley and Fats and their retinues stood aside, taking no part in this concluding formality. The inspector and his boys also stood aside watching the people they had come to see. To the words he had from each person in turn the old guy's responses were never more than perfunctory. Thanks for people's sympathy came from his son who kept trying to cover for his father's ungraciousness and who drew baleful looks from the old man for his pains.

When I reached the wheelchair and spoke my name, I was shouted down before I could more than begin on my words of sympathy.

"Never mind about how sorry you are," the old man said, broadcasting at what was evidently his standard decibel level. "You're his detective friend. When are you going to stop talking and find me his murderer?"

"I'm not," I said, and that was as far as I got.

"Don't tell me what you're not." He shouted me down again. "I know who you are and what you are. Lansing used to speak of you. I want you to find his killer. I want you to make him try to escape. You are going to make him try, and you are going to fill him full of lead. You are going to do that because I want him dead. I don't want life imprisonment and parole and all that soft-headed nonsense. An eye for an eye. I want him shot down and killed. I don't want some smart lawyer getting him off."

To offer any argument against these notions of justice was so obviously futile that I had no thought of attempting it. The simple assertion that I was just as much the private citizen as he was himself was the limit of what I was going for. I might just as well have skipped even that much effort. The old curmudgeon was not a listener. He heard nothing but the sound of his own voice, if even that. He had a mind so securely tied to its preconceived notions that nothing so trivial as a fact could ever penetrate it.

I had no more than opened my mouth before he was telling me off again. "I have made you aware of my position," he said. "There are people waiting behind you. You are holding them up. Move on and let me get this over with."

I know when I'm licked. I moved on. I had from the son a small placating smile and a smaller apologetic shrug. Since for both he found it necessary to make some small adjustment to the wheelchair which put him safely behind his father's back, I held off on any response that might have given him away. I had moved off securely beyond the old tyrant's line of vision before I sketched in for the younger man my own small smile and shrug.

Inspector Schmidt moved in and took me in tow. "See anyone here who means anything?" he asked.

"Smiley and Fats and their troops," I said.

"For them I don't depend on you, kid."

"Otherwise the few guys from the club. On the couples I draw a blank. They all look like money, but you can see that for yourself."

"The fellows you know—were any of them closer to him than you were?"

"Could be," I said. "I should be picking up on that in the next few days just from the talk there'll be in the locker room and along the bar."

"You'll give me the word?"

I squirmed. "Police spy? *Agent provacateur?*"

Schmitty grinned. "Don't build it that big. You're just a guy who loves gossip and can't stop yourself from passing it on to a friend. If you want something that sounds more impressive, you're a good citizen."

"I'll give you this much, Schmitty," I said. "You're not asking as much as his uncle, but—damn it all—you don't need it. You know where to look. It's Fats or Smiley, one or the other."

"Yeah, except that I was watching them all through the service and something doesn't fit."

"I had the impression—and after all, I had it from you—that if there's anything going on around here that isn't run by Smiley, it's run by Fats."

"That's the picture I've had, and it's been my hunch it's also the picture they've had."

"What does that mean?"

"Okay, Baggy. Ordinarily I don't feel at all close to those two babies, but this morning I do. Of course, it's only a gut feeling."

"You've always had reliable guts. So what are they feeling?"

"I've seen too many of these things and they've always run to type," the inspector said. "There's the general whose man has been knocked off. He buries the church in flowers and he shows at the

funeral. That's the least of what he's going to do for the dead man.
Then there's the general who ordered the killing. He sends even
more flowers and he's there among the mourners. I've never known
who he thinks he's fooling. Maybe he hopes it'll be me, but more
likely it's just good murderer's manners, not expected to fool anyone."

"So what doesn't fit?" I asked. "You couldn't ask for more
flowers, and the two of them came."

"It's something in the way they're acting. They aren't watching
each other. They're both of them watching those guys you know
from your club. My hunch is that they've begun to think someone
new is moving in on the territory, and they came to try to get a line
on who."

I thought I had a hold on what he was thinking, but I just
couldn't believe it.

"And you're thinking that if I listen along the bar and in the
locker room, I'll come up with this line you want?"

"It's one possibility."

"Oh come on! A solid, respectable citizen, a guy I may have been
drinking with, a guy I may even have lost to at squash, is running
himself another life of gang-lording?"

"You didn't believe it of the late Lansing Monroe, every man's
friend," the inspector said.

"All right. I admit it. I didn't. But in his case at least I always felt
there was something phony about the man."

"And another man may be a better actor," Schmitty said.

You must be thinking that for all this talk we'd been a long time
hanging on in front of the church. We were. All the people who
had lined up to offer their words of sympathy had done their duty,
collected the old man's ungracious responses, and taken off. Some
of the talk, however, had continued after we'd left the church.

I'd had no intention of following the coffin out to the cemetery
for the graveside do; but, since Schmitty and his boys were going
and we'd been at some specially provocative point in our discussion
when the cortege was taking off, I rode along with the inspector.
Brimming over with questions, I could do no less.

It was a most extraordinary funeral procession. So far as I could see no provision had been made for anyone to go to the graveside except uncle and cousin. There was only their car and one for the minister. It could have been that all other cars had been preempted for the great overflow of flowers, but it seemed more likely that those additional cars had been hastily ordered up after the deluge.

Everyone else who followed was providing his own transportation. I rode with the inspector in his car, and his men were in their unmarked police vehicles. We brought up the rear of the procession since it was only on a last-minute decision that we tagged on.

None of the gang from the club was going and none of the couples who had come to the church. It was when Fats and his minions began lining their cars up to fall into line that the inspector gave his orders. Fats was not to go to the grave without a police escort. Smiley, however, was not far behind. He and his cohorts were falling into line behind the Fats Jenkins gang. We brought up the rear.

I've already reported the exchange I had with the inspector, much of which took place on the way to the cemetery. I did interrupt it briefly for one question.

"Isn't this graveside business excessive?" I asked.

"This whole thing is out of whack," Inspector Schmidt said.

At graveside it was indeed out of whack. For the brief burial service uncle and his son were there alone. Everyone else stayed back, keeping their distance. The police contingent, and I along with them, stood back as well. We hadn't come for the burial. We had come to watch those two peculiar bands of mourners.

The coffin was lowered into the grave and the flowers were mounded high above it. Uncle and son returned to their car and sped away. The rest of us still lingered. There were several moments of mounting tension with each of the two groups eyeing the other warily. Then suddenly it broke. Smiley Donohue moved toward the grave. Fats Jenkins matched him move for move. They were shoulder to shoulder when they went plowing into the flowers. The inspector grinned.

"If that's all they wanted," he said, "I could have told them. There are no cards. I had a man at the church early to check. All the flowers were sent anonymously."

CHAPTER 3

At the thought of doing what Inspector Schmidt was asking of me I was of a complicated state of mind. A more honest word for it might have been confused. Those guys at the club, since they had always considered me one of them, would trust me. To come among them behind a screen of friendly companionship and operate as a spy and informer was distasteful.

On the other hand a man had been murdered. I could tell myself that any murderer, just by the act of killing, cuts himself away from all the civilized rules, sets himself outside all practices of civility. Even then I found for myself an evasion. I suggested that Schmitty come to dinner at the club and that we spend the evening there. He could do his own probing and his own listening. It wasn't going to be his first time there. He had been there with me on several previous occasions. The fellows knew who he was.

We gave it the full treatment, beginning in the late afternoon when the squash players would be on hand. There was no chance of a game since I hadn't reserved a court, but it didn't matter. Squash would have been out in any case. Inspector Schmidt reserves his energies for his professional activities.

"I can do without little boys' games," he says whenever the subject comes up. "The games killers play give me all the exercise I need."

He did go for a quick swim, just one length of the pool and back, but even that was in line of duty. It gave him entree to the relaxed locker-room companionship of shared dripping nudity. The inspector was a rousing locker-room success.

When over a long period of time the same guys shower and dress together day after day the standard routine of rough horseplay and jovial obscenity becomes too standard. Schmitty brought novelty and fresh invention to both. He was the star of the afternoon. He was hardly out from under the shower before he had himself firmly established as one of the boys.

We had dinner and spent a long evening. With the inspector as the stellar attraction, the club bar did great business that night. Ordinarily people start drifting off shortly after dinner if they have even stayed on to dinner. Most evenings the commuters drop in only for a drink or two before they run for their trains. That night just about everybody stayed on until the bar closed, and even then people ordered last drinks and loitered over them long after the barmen had packed it in.

The guys who had been at the church that morning were all there. They formed the nucleus of the group that gathered around Schmitty. It seemed to me that they kept asking him questions and they were telling him nothing. I had the annoyance of three or four interruptions in the course of the evening. I would be called to the phone, and when I picked it up I'd find myself on a dead line. I got sick of it, and I told the man on the switchboard to get a name before he called me to the phone again. That put an end to it. When we were leaving the club, however, the doorman told me that there had been another call and when asked for his name, the caller had hung up. Despite all the interruptions, I missed nothing. Schmitty assured me of that.

All these guys who were pumping the inspector were baffled. Everyone was full of curiosity and looking to the inspector for a fill-in on the inside dope. He was the expert. He would have access to information they didn't have. Had he learned anything? Had he any ideas? What did he think of it?

"The uncle," Schmitty said. "What can anybody think of that old bastard?"

"Senile." That came from one of the fellows who had witnessed the performance in the church.

"Ugly senile," another of the guys said.

"It seems to me," Schmitty said, "it's what a man has been all his life. The difference is that when they get old they lose control of it, and everything that's always been wrong with them surfaces."

Someone recalled times when Monroe had talked about his uncle. The consensus was that he had been fond of the old man, had spoken of him with warmth and admiration.

"We've picked up something funny on that," Schmitty said. "Monroe had the papers in for a legal change of name. He was waiting for a hearing on it. He was going to take his mother's maiden name. He wanted to be Lansing Monroe McLeod. It could be he liked uncle that much, or maybe he didn't like his father."

Nobody was disposed to pick up on that. What the boys wanted from the inspector was not any theorizing about the peculiarities of family ties.

"All of those guys that came." One of the boys was trying it from another angle. "They looked as though they didn't belong and they acted that way too. Afterward none of them made a move to talk to the old man."

Another fellow picked up on it. "And it wasn't that they could have been afraid of him," he said. "They looked tough, too tough to be scared of anyone."

"If you noticed the guns under their jackets," the inspector said, "they were just on the job. They were my men."

"Not the fat one. He looked like an overweight baby, hardened and multiplied."

"Yes. Him and Scarface, the one with the frozen half a smile."

"And all the smoothies that were hanging around them. Slick smooth. Too smooth and too tough."

"Them," Schmitty said. "They were the reason I had my people there. It was to keep an eye on them. You don't want a gang war breaking out across the coffin. Uncle wouldn't have liked that. As it was, they behaved. They'd just come to see the flowers."

"The flowers. Weren't they something?"

Schmitty shrugged it off. "They always are at a gangster's funeral," he said.

That produced shock and it seemed to be universal. If anyone was counterfeiting it, I couldn't detect it.

"Gangster?"

"Lansing?"

"Come on, Inspector. He was a member here."

"He was machine-gunned, just about cut in half by it. That isn't done except in war, and that includes gang war. It's not the way jealous wives do it. It's not the way muggers do it. Machine guns are gangster stuff."

There were several moments of silence while the boys were digesting that. The guy who had asserted club membership as a guarantee of honest respectability was the first to come out of shock.

"It doesn't have to mean he belonged," he said. "What about a good citizen who gets onto something and they kill him to stop him going to the DA with it."

"No."

"Why not? It's been known to happen, hasn't it?"

"Gangs," the inspector said, "are business organizations. Their methods of operation are businesslike. Any day now I expect I'll be seeing murder computerized."

"Isn't it good business to silence a man who, if left alive, is going to put them out of business?"

"Silence him, yes, but not with a machine gun. As in any business, there are operations that should be publicized and some that are better kept under cover."

The inspector explained that. In gang warfare the gang wants its killing to carry something you might call the gang signature. A member of the rival gang is bumped. It is important that the rival gang make no mistake. You are not going to terrorize that rival gang if you let your killing slip away from you, permitting any doubt to arise about where it should be credited.

"That's the story on Monroe's murder," he said. "It was done in the killing-of-a-member-of-a-rival-gang pattern. A citizen outside any gang operation becomes a threat to them and they have to eliminate him. Okay, they'll bump him, but not this way. They won't put the gang signature on it. They don't open up any line of thought that will go: Here we have a good citizen. If a gang erased him, it must have been because he had something on them. That will start us looking for what he might have had. They don't invite that."

The bar was closed and even those last drinks served just before the barmen packed it in had been finished. People began heading for home. The inspector and I waited it out until the last of the diehards had gone. I couldn't see that there had been anything in the evening for Inspector Schmidt but the brief swim, the dinner, and some drinks. I could, however, find nothing in his manner to indicate that he was disappointed. I asked him.

"If you are looking for me to tell you that one of your buddies did or said anything to give himself away," Schmitty said, "he didn't."

"So that's a dead end," I said.

"Probably. A guy would have to be a great actor to carry it off the way all of them did, and more than that, he'd have to have enormous confidence in his acting ability even to have tried it."

"So why only probably? All the guys who came to the funeral you saw here tonight."

"Is it dead sure that the man I want came to the funeral?"

"Don't gangsters always?"

"It's customary, but this is an odd one. I've been adding up all the oddities."

He lined them up for me. The flowers had been sent anonymously. The inspector had ordered a check run on florists. They had come from a shop that had no gang connections. They had been ordered by telephone and payment had been made in cash. The florist had not seen the man who made the order and had no clue to his identity.

"That florist may have no gang connections," I said, "but, if he hasn't been bought, he's been frightened into telling the required lies."

"What's your thinking on that?" the inspector asked.

"All those flowers bought at retail—or even at wholesale for that matter—it's a fortune. That kind of money entrusted to a messenger? So how come he didn't see the buyer?"

"Yes, of course. That had to be checked out. It's another one of the oddities. The order was made by phone. The florist was prom-

ised payment in cash well before it would be time for delivery.
Sure enough, the payment was made and in no more than ten
minutes."

"How?"

"A fat envelope of bills pushed through the mail slot in the shop
door. When the florist opened it up and saw what it was, he did
look out. Who wouldn't be curious? So he remained curious. All he
could see was the usual New York scene, street full of people hurrying by, going about their business."

"You got the envelope from him?"

"Not a chance. He had destroyed it."

"Maybe you should be taking another good look at him," I said.
"Anything that peculiar, wouldn't you think he would have kept
it?"

"Average law-abiding business man," the inspector said. "Given
a good enough temptation, a touch of larceny gets to him. He's no
good at it. He's inexperienced, and even while he's doing it, he's
scared of what he's doing. A big sale like that and it's ready-made
for sales-tax and income-tax concealment. All he has to do is keep
no record of it, not even the envelope the money came in. He didn't
expect that the police would be around to question him about it,
and since he's no kind of an old hand at anything even as mildly illegal as tax evasion, it took no more than our turning up for him to
come apart. He reads like a book—too easy."

"How did you find him? You mean just the sight of your boys
scared him so bad that he didn't even try to pretend he wasn't the
florist who'd filled the order?"

"He couldn't. We knew we had the right store and the boys let
him know straight off that we knew and how we knew."

"So why not cue me in? How?"

"The people at the church know him. As it happens, he's the
friendly neighborhood florist for a lot of their parishioners. He's
done flowers a lot of times in the church, for weddings and fu-
nerals. The people at the church know his truck and know his men.
That was all the asking around the boys had to do."

"That should make it a fancy shop in an upper-upper neighborhood," I said.

"A neighborhood where people like your club buddies live."

He went back to adding up the oddities. Ordinarily flowers at a gang funeral come from two gangs, the bereaved gang and the one responsible for the killing. Not infrequently when the gang situation is more crowded and complex and there are tensions going in an assortment of directions there will be flowers from even more gangs. Lansing Monroe's flowers, easily abundant enough to have been the offerings of at least two, had been curiously different. They had, every last blossom, leaf, and thorn, come from the single anonymous donor.

"It still looks like a gang deal," Inspector Schmidt said, "but if it is, it has to be a new man come into the territory without either Fats or Smiley knowing about him yet. I can understand his wanting to keep it that way for as long as he can manage it. That could be the why of the anonymity on the flowers, and it would be why he might not have shown at the church. I can find an explanation for all that."

His tone was saying there was more.

"Then what can't you explain?" I asked.

"Who Monroe was and where he belonged. He didn't belong to Fats and he didn't belong to Smiley. They were both at the funeral to explore a situation that had them baffled. That much I'm certain of. So this new man in the territory murdered him or had him murdered, but he had to belong somewhere. Two new gangs moving into the territory? Nobody's had even the first word, not us, not Smiley, not Fats. How the hell can that be happening?"

"This may be more of a story than you thought," I said.

"Could be," the inspector said. "One thing for sure, it's more of a headache. We've got one thing though that maybe can do us some good."

"What's that?"

"You guys here at the club—you're good, stout drinkers."

"Some more, some less," I said. "What's that got to do with anything?"

"What's the score on cocaine?"

"Here at the club? Nothing I've ever seen or heard of."

"It's the fashionable drug and you're a tony bunch."

"If any of them are into it, they're doing it other places. I'd say our regulars are fellows who had their vices firmly established before cocaine became fashionable. What's the connection, Schmitty?"

"Monroe."

"That much I could guess, but aren't you reaching?"

"Right now it's the best lead I've got."

"Just picked it out of the air?"

"A lot better than that. This afternoon Narcotics picked up a guy. He was selling. Name's Oliver Williams. Male nurse. Currently unemployed. Most recent employer was Josiah McLeod. Ollie is telling the Narcs that he has no supplier because his supplier used to be Lansing Monroe and Monroe's been shot out from under him."

"They believing him?" I asked because I wasn't.

"You're thinking it's too convenient?"

"Isn't it? The guy doesn't want to sing and he thinks luck has handed him an easy out. His former employer's nephew has just been gunned down. If he has to hand someone to the Narcs, why not this all too convenient dead man? It's better than refusing to talk."

Schmitty nodded. "That," he said, "is what they're thinking over at Narcotics. I'm not saying it isn't the way it is, but after all Monroe was messing around with someone who does business with a machine gun. Do you think it was some gentleman who was sore at losing to Monroe at squash?"

I shut up. I didn't know what to think. It was the inspector's headache.

Leaving the club, Schmitty was going to headquarters to clear his desk. He offered to run me home first, but it was a beautiful night and I'd had an evening of a little too much to drink and far too much cigarette smoke. It's only a short walk and I wanted the air. You've heard about the dangers of the New York streets and you undoubtedly have a picture of a mugger at every corner and between the corners. There are muggers, of course, but they aren't all that many. On the averages you're not the one who will get hit. I've lived in New York all my life, and if you are a New Yorker, you live by the averages. Don't you do that anywhere?

I had my walk and the averages were with me. I enjoyed the freshness of the cool night air. I cleared my lungs and made some small headway toward clearing my head. If there were any muggers about, they were having none of me. I was turning into my street and all but home before anything happened to break the peace and quiet.

It was just a car. It came careening down the street at a speed I thought conceivable only for a maniac or a drunk. Even as I was having that thought, however, I was amending it to include Inspector Schmidt on urgent business. The car whisked around the corner. A second car came roaring after it, and only a split second after the second car had also disappeared around the corner I heard a few quick shots. I ran back to the avenue to have a look. By the time I got there, everything was again quiet. Both cars were gone.

I turned about and headed back home, but then it was only as far as my doorstep. My front door stood slightly ajar and I remembered the calls I'd been having through the evening. I knew better than to go in. I told you I go with the averages.

CHAPTER 4

I zipped back to the street corner and dialed the local precinct from the booth there. I got through to the desk sergeant and it was almost no time at all before a squad car picked me up at the phone booth.

"You were quick," I said.

"We were right in close when your call came through. We been getting calls from people, they was woke up by a shot. So we been out looking. Nobody but you around. No dead body. No blood. Nothing. You been doing any shooting, Mr. Bagby?"

"No," I said. "I thought it was you."

Their question had been asked in jest. My response threw them. "Us shooting?"

I told them about the car chase and the shot I'd heard. In combination with my open door, that had now taken on an interest it hadn't had before. If it hadn't been police pursuit and a warning shot, what could it have been?

"Skylarking drunks," one of the two cops said.

"Or feuding and fussing," the other one offered.

It was left at that when we reached my apartment door. I should explain that I live in a converted town house that was divided into apartments. Mine is on the ground floor. You enter it directly from the street.

The boys insisted that I stay outside on the doorstep while they went in to explore. It was a considerable time that I was waiting. For my bachelor needs the apartment is spacious but it is no enormous complex of rooms—just a large living room with bar and din-

ing area, the bedroom, study, kitchen, and bath. I could guess that
the boys were being thorough. At the rear the apartment has access
to a garden. It is a large garden maintained jointly by all the people
whose houses and apartments back on to it. Searching its paths and
thickets of shrubbery against the possibility of some lurking intruder would be taking much of the time.

Eventually they came back out.

"It's all right, Mr. Bagby," one of them said. "You can come in."

"You maybe can think it's all right," the other one said. "Mr.
Bagby won't. He's got one hell of a mess in there."

I was no more than inside the door when I was confronted with
what I was to see were only minor indications of a hell of a mess.
The cops had turned on all the lights and even out in the entrance
hall the devastation was obvious. I enjoy pictures and they hang everywhere in the apartment. The drawings and prints were all off
the entrance-hall walls. They lay face down on the floor with the
backing paper that sealed the frames slashed and ripped away.

That was nothing to what had been done in the other rooms. Pictures everywhere had been similarly treated. All upholstery had
been slashed and the stuffing pulled out and dumped on the floor.
In like manner in the bedroom the mattresses and pillows had been
gutted. All the books throughout the apartment had been pulled off
the shelves. They were piled everywhere in disorderly heaps. Every
drawer in the place had been pulled out and its contents dumped.
In the closets my suits and slacks had been pulled off the hangers
and they lay on the floor with every pocket turned out.

Then there was the paper. If you know anything about writers,
you should know that we drown in paper. What with manuscripts,
notes, correspondence, and contracts, we live constantly on the
edge of being snowed under. It's sufficiently overwhelming when
you keep it neatly stacked. Dumped and scattered, it suffers a di-
sastrous multiplication in bulk.

Just moving around in the apartment took a lot of doing. The
place was hip deep in stuff. It took miracles of navigation to pick
your way between the disorderly piles. It was obvious that it would
be a long time and much work before I could hope to determine
what had been taken. Even the kitchen had been given the treat-

ment. All the dishes and glassware, all the pots and pans had been moved out of the cupboards and the shelf paper had been ripped from the shelves. The drawers of the kitchen cabinets had been dumped just as were the drawers in the other rooms, but here there was a difference. I noticed it at once and it seemed a crazy difference.

In the other rooms the lining paper that had been in the drawers was dumped along with everything else they'd contained. I had taken no particular notice of that. If you empty a drawer by upending it, that is going to happen. In the kitchen drawers, however, the lining paper hadn't been loose. It had been securely pasted in. What might have seemed merely incidental elsewhere, here was unmistakably deliberate. This lining paper had been gouged with a knife point and ripped away from the drawer in ribbons.

It was in the kitchen that I first had glimmerings of the thought that I might have been hit not so much by a burglar as by a vandal. The ravaged lining paper seemed evidence of it, strong evidence in combination with the fact that even a quick look at the dumped silver showed me that none of it had been taken. A burglar so illiterate that he cannot read the Sterling mark?

I picked my way back to the bedroom for another look in the closets. On my first look there I hadn't thought about luggage. Now I was thinking in terms of what I knew to be a standard operating procedure for burglars. There are those who go exclusively for money or jewelry. I wasn't concerned about that type. Money that isn't in the bank I carry on my person, and there is never any great amount of that. In this age of charge cards and payment by check, small amounts for taxis, tips, and minor purchases are all that can ever be needed. I never have cash stowed away in the apartment. Jewelry amounts to little more than watch and cuff links, and those I had on me.

Another breed concentrates on typewriters, TVs, and record players. Even in passing I had seen that all of those were *in situ*. The burglar who takes clothes or other such items of some bulk, that will be conspicuous when carried through the streets, will, if he can find any, also take luggage. A man can appear with a couple of suitcases and hope to pass unchallenged. Those heaps of stuff all over the place were stacked so large that I was finding it hard to believe that, when I had them sorted out, I wouldn't find everything I owned. In all that wild disorder, however, I had no way of knowing.

All my luggage was there. It had been taken off the closet shelves and it lay opened on the floor. There were two suitcases that had combination locks. Those had been forced open.

I had come that far in my tour of inspection when Inspector Schmidt turned up. I could imagine no reason for his appearing at that time of night unless he'd had some staggering new development in the Lansing Monroe killing. I was thinking he was about to go somewhere to make some move on it and wanted me with him.

"Now what's happened?" I asked.

"You tell me," he said.

"Here? You can see for yourself."

"I sure enough can."

"I mean what brings you around?"

"This," the inspector said.

"This? How did you know?"

"Report came to my desk. Even this time of night we have boys smart enough to add two and two."

"That makes them smarter than me."

"You haven't worked it out? Not at all?"

"I've had a burglar," I said. "It's too soon to tell. I can't possibly know until I have this whole mess sorted out and put together again. So far it looks like a crazy burglar, more destructive than larcenous. So I'm still asking. Since when are they rushing burglary reports to Homicide?"

"This isn't just any burglary report," Schmitty said. "This one may add up."

He did the sum for me. The boys knew the inspector had a murder and the victim was a man I'd known. They get a report of gunfire complaints and the complaints come from my street. They may not register on that connection immediately. After all, just off the top of their heads they wouldn't have known my address. Then, however, it is followed by another report. This one is of a burglary in my apartment and the report includes the apartment address. With that the thing starts coming together for them.

Questions arise. Can gunshot and burglary be unrelated events? Can both bear no relation to the murder of the man George Bagby knew? Even if they might be only remotely related to a murder, questions like that go straight to Inspector Schmidt.

Because there is the big garden at the back, my apartment is laid out with living room and bedroom at the rear where it is quiet and beautiful. Kitchen and bathroom are at the street side. Coming in off the street, therefore, you go past the kitchen before hitting any of the rest of it except the entrance hall. Coming into the kitchen, the inspector picked up one of the empty drawers. He took a hard look at the gouged lining paper and then turned to look at the other emptied drawers.

"It's a stupid question," he said, "but do you have any sort of an idea of what may be missing?"

"Even if I could think of something," I said, "I wouldn't know that it isn't here, buried under one pileup or another."

"Big things? Typewriter? TV? Stereo?"

"All here."

"Okay. Kitchen's a good test. A burglar takes a kitchen apart looking for silver or for money stashed away in something like a teapot. What about the silver?"

"Dumped out of the drawers, but it's all here. I've checked."

Saying nothing, Schmitty left the kitchen. He hit the bedroom next. After just the first quick look he picked his way between the piles of stuff to the bedside table. I have a telephone extension there. Making a quick call, he snapped out orders. He was having a man sent over to stand guard on the apartment. I couldn't understand that. It struck me as the proverbial locking the barn door after the horse had been stolen even though it might very well have been that the horse was still there buried in the chaotic jumble.

Hanging up the phone, he turned back to me. "You've got a big job ahead of you," he said, "getting this place fixed up again."

"You haven't seen the worst of it," I said. "The living room. The books. All my papers."

"Uhhuh." He was squatted down, taking a close look at the

empty suitcases. I didn't know whether or not he was listening to me. For the moment he seemed to be elsewhere. I squatted down beside him and he showed me something that I had failed to notice. In all the cases the linings had been ripped loose. I was well past being impressed by a little thing like that. It couldn't loom large in the context of the slashed and gutted upholstery and the slashed and gutted mattresses.

"That's just more of the same," I said. "As far as I can make out, I didn't have a burglar. I had some kind of a crazy vandal."

The inspector had come up out of his squat and was looking at the mattresses.

"You'll need a bed," he said. "There isn't much left of the night, but even for what there is, you'll want to do better than the sofa out in your living room."

"The sofa and the easy chairs are all as thoroughly disemboweled as the mattresses and pillows," I said.

We moved on to the living room. The inspector stopped short in the doorway. He should have been prepared for the look of it, but no one could have been prepared for those overwhelming drifts of paper.

"It's no good your trying to deal with this tonight," he said. "You'll spend the night in my place."

"I can get a room at the club."

The inspector has a spare bed, as do I. There have been countless times when he's had me along on an investigation where things are moving fast and the two of us have stayed together twenty-four hours a day, both of us using his apartment or mine when we can grab off a few hours for sleep. This time I demurred because it seemed to me that the occasion was slightly different. I couldn't see it as a job-related necessity.

"Head in the lion's mouth?" Schmitty said. "Do you like it in there?"

"What does that mean?"

"Look around you, Baggy. This guy was interrupted. He had to quit before he had finished here."

"Not finished? What more could he have done? Burned the house down?"

"He wouldn't have wanted to do that except maybe as a last resort," Inspector Schmidt said, and for the moment he left it there.

It was just then that the man who was to stand guard arrived. The inspector broke off to give him his instructions. We were in his car, headed for his apartment and bed, before I could get a fuller explanation.

"You didn't have a crazy vandal," he said. "Crazy is always the easy out when something isn't readily explained. There's always a reason. It may be a crazy reason with its own left-field logic, but you don't get far in this business unless you look for the reason and try to understand the logic of it."

"So what's the logic?"

"The guy is a burglar who wanted only one thing. He knew exactly what he wanted and he was interested in nothing else. What he was looking for was something flat—something that could be hidden in a book, hidden under the backing on a picture, tucked away in a mattress or in upholstery, hidden under shelf paper or under the lining paper in a drawer, tucked away among a lot of papers that had nothing to do with it, hidden under the lining of a suitcase. Okay. So what is it that can be hidden in a place like any of those?"

"A paper?"

"Obviously."

"Paper is the most of anything I've got, but nothing that could be of any possible use or even interest to anyone but myself."

"Very likely," the inspector said, "but you may not know. Since he was interrupted before he had finished, if there is anything, the odds are that it's still there. You'll want to be thinking of that when you get to putting the papers in order. There just might be something."

I was absolutely certain that there would be nothing. It was no use arguing that. The inspector had already said that I might not know. I had a question and I preferred to push that.

"You keep saying he was interrupted before he had finished. What more was there that he could possibly have done?"

"Ripped the wallpaper off the walls. He probably wouldn't have risked digging up the garden. Remember the car chase and the gunfire? What could all that have been if it wasn't some sort of interruption?"

"But my papers," I said. "I know what I have there. You're assuming that there's something and that it's so terrifically important to someone that it would make him go to all that trouble and risk. You're assuming this guy knows the significance of some paper or papers I have, and I don't. That's one place I can tell you you're wrong."

"Okay," the inspector said. "What he was looking for isn't there, wasn't there, and never has been there. All the same, it's easy to understand that people can be thinking there is something and that you would have it carefully hidden away."

"What people?" I asked. "And on what basis?"

"You were Monroe's detective friend."

"Nobody believes that but one crazy old man."

"He announced it and there was nobody at the funeral who could have missed hearing it. Then riding out to the cemetery you rode with me. That must have looked like confirmation. So it's given people ideas."

He sketched out these possible ideas for me. He told me I had to take into account the natural cynicism of the mob. A man has gang involvement and he also has a detective friend. It is the immediate assumption that the detective is more than a friend. He's a collaborator.

I picked up on it. I could see what would follow, and it seemed so silly that I was impatient to knock it down.

"So Monroe knows there's a contract out on him," I said. "He writes a letter telling all he knows about Fats or Smiley, whichever, and he gives it to his detective friend with the instruction to keep it hidden in some safe place and open it only if something violent should happen to him."

"That would be the picture," the inspector said. "Who would have been more likely for Monroe to have picked for the duty than his crooked cop friend?"

"Leaving out the fact that this would be going way out on nothing more than a tremendous string of the thinnest assumptions, there's still one big thing that tears it. If I had any such letter, why wouldn't I have already brought it out of hiding, read it, and turned it over to you? How could even an idiot think I would still be holding it, that it was still hidden away in the apartment?"

"That part of the thinking wouldn't be too bad. Nothing has happened. Obviously it would be silly to expect that nothing was going to happen. The question would be why you were holding off. Since you're a crooked cop, you're not interested in justice. You're dedicated to making the big buck. You're holding it while you're working out a way to use it."

"One more question," I said. "Since it wasn't the department, what was the interruption? Who was chasing the guy? Who shot at him?"

"Three possibilities. If we knew who it was who worked your place over, it would perhaps narrow down to two: in the apartment it could have been someone who belongs to Fats or a Smiley man or, if there is some unknown third force moving in, someone out of that gang. Depending on which one was inside, the chasing and the shooting would have been done by one or another of the other two."

Crazy as it was, I had to accept it as a better answer than anything I could have thought up. I recognized that it was in line with the inspector's way of thinking. For every event there would be a logical reason. If it should be a crazy event, it might be a crazy reason supported by its own mad logic.

CHAPTER 5

I can't say that by light of day my wrecked apartment looked any worse than it had during the night. It couldn't. If it seemed that way, it was only because I was now confronted with the immediate necessity for getting down to the job of bringing order out of the overwhelming chaos. For one wild moment I was tempted to put a match to it and walk away, but you can't commit arson when you have a police guard standing alongside you.

I picked up the phone. My first call was to the insurance agent to alert him to the granddaddy of all claims I would be throwing at him as soon as I could assess the damage. Next I called something that calls itself a sleep shop. They had a pair of mattresses that were duplicates of my wrecked ones. They promised to get them delivered to me before the day was over. I also ordered replacements for the gutted pillows.

I called an upholsterer who had done some repair work for me. He was a neighborhood man and he said he'd come right around to see what could be done and how much could be salvaged.

"Nothing can be salvaged," I said.

The cop had been waiting to talk to me. He told me that the technical men had been in and had finished their work. They'd left me a message.

"They'll be reporting to the inspector," he said, "but they thought you'd maybe want to get started on getting fixed up."

"In what way?" I asked.

"The guy got in too easy. He just climbed in your kitchen window. You had ought to at least keep that window locked when you go out. It's too easy from the street, ground floor and all. The guys say you really need bars put on the window. Any ground-floor window to the street, it had ought to have bars on it."

"I've been resisting thinking it," I said. "It's the criminals who should be behind bars, not me."

"That's for sure, but what can you do? Ground floor, street side, it just ain't safe." He brought a folded piece of paper out of his tunic pocket. "If you want," he said, "this guy does a good job."

So then I had another number to call, only to learn that the inspector had already called the man and he was even then on his way over.

Fresh out of excuses for stalling, I took off my coat and shirt, preparing to get started. The telephone bell promised another reprieve. It was the inspector. He began by telling me he had the man coming around to bar the window. Since I was now in the apartment, he was pulling the guard off, but I wasn't to leave the place even briefly without calling precinct. He had them alerted. They would send a man around to hold the fort any time I would be gone.

"We'll do that till the bars are on the window," he said.

"You think he'll be back?"

"If I read him right, he won't. We're doing it anyhow, just in case I'm not reading him right."

"You've lost me, Schmitty."

"Simple enough. If he was coming back to finish the job . . ."

I broke in. "I know," I said. "He can hardly try to dig up the garden by daylight."

"I never really thought he'd do that, much as he might want to, but there is the wallpaper. No. I'm thinking that if he was coming back, it would have been before now. By now he should be feeling very sure that anything you might have had there won't be there any longer. After last night you'd have removed it. If you do find anything, you'll lose no time about getting it out of the apartment, won't you?"

"I'd hand it right over to you," I said. "But then I'm not interested in making the big buck out of it."

"If you were, what would you do with it after last night?"

"I see what you mean."

"You'd rush it into a bank vault or such, wouldn't you?"

"Right."

"Have you begun clearing up yet?"

"Just about to start when you called."

"I'd like you to begin with the papers. Don't make any assumptions. It'll drive you crazy, but the only way to do it is if you look at every sheet."

"It'll drive me crazy, but I'll do it. You'll have to pay for the straitjacket."

"I'll have one made to order for you and by the best tailor in town. Meanwhile put the officer on and get to it."

I had no sooner than begun with the papers than I realized that I was going to have to do them as Schmitty wanted them done. They were in such a jumble of wild disorder that nothing I picked up belonged with anything else in its vicinity. Unless I looked at each individual sheet and sorted them into piles and then arranged the piles in proper coherent order, I would never again be able to find anything I needed.

I had no lack of cleared flat surfaces on which to stack and sort them. There was the top of the bar and there were all the emptied bookshelves. The cop was on the phone only briefly before he pulled out.

With every sheet of paper I looked at I fell into deeper discouragement. Compared to the job I had on my hands, the labors of Hercules were idleness. If it hadn't been for Inspector Schmidt's demands, I would have quickly given up on it, just bundled the whole mess together, leaving the sorting out to be done in reasonably brief sessions. I kept thinking of something like an hour a day for the rest of my life.

I stayed with it till one o'clock when I took off to grab myself some lunch. There was bread and the refrigerator gave me milk and butter and cheese. There was also some fruit. I piled all of it on a tray and picked my way out of the kitchen. I perched on a bar stool and ate my lunch. I had just taken my first drag on my after-luncheon cigarette when the doorbell rang. Expecting the man with the kitchen-window bars, I went to the door.

The man was out there, but he was only just pulling up in his truck. On the doorstep I had a caller. My first thought was that this would be something new in the lexicon of good manners, a condolence call in reverse. My visitor was Josiah McLeod, Jr. I recognized him from the funeral the previous day and I had also seen him occasionally around the club with Lansing Monroe. I knew his name from the newspaper obits. He was the cousin, listed along with his father, Josiah McLeod, as the surviving relatives of Lansing Monroe.

"Mr. Bagby," he said. "I had to come around and apologize for my father."

The wrought-iron man was off his truck and coming up behind McLeod.

"Excuse me a moment," I said. "I have to take care of this."

"It's all right," he said. "No hurry."

The man who had come about the window bars explained that he had been around earlier, before I'd gotten back from Schmitty's. He had measured the window. He now had in his truck a few sets of bars of different design. They were all of a size to fit the window. If I would just take a look at them and make a choice, he would get right along with the job. I looked along the row of house fronts and noticed something I had previously been ignoring. Several of them had bars fitted to their ground-floor windows and all the bars were of like design. It occurred to me that there might be an agreement that demanded uniformity and I hadn't checked on it.

It was no problem. One of the designs he had brought along matched those others. I chose that one. He approved my choice. I left him to it.

McLeod was still on the doorstep, waiting.

"Sorry," I said. "I had to get him started."

"It's all right. I can wait."

"You have nothing to apologize for, Mr. McLeod."

"He is my father."

"An old man, and he isn't the first old man to be difficult. It's something you just ride with. People understand."

"You're being great about it."

"Nonsense. He just got things wrong end to. The old often do. I should have left it alone. I don't know why I tried to straighten him out. I knew better. Old people, if they take a position, nothing can ever move them off it. They just can't admit that they might be wrong about anything. The crux of it is that they can't admit it to themselves because it tells them they are slipping. That's what makes them dig in their heels over even the most trifling things, and it's what makes them so irascible about it."

McLeod laughed. It was one of those painfully mirthless laughs. "Mr. Bagby," he said, "you sound as if you'd been living with my old man except that it doesn't take even a trifle to make him irascible. He just is. He always has been."

"Want some advice, Mr. McLeod?" I said.

"Call me Joe."

I laughed. "If I'm presuming to give advice," I said, "I suppose Joe would have the more suitable sound. It's easy to see that you're having the roughest sort of time. Don't add to it by taking on anything that isn't yours. Just leave it that people will understand about your father. If they don't understand, so what? They'll resent the old man. Is that going to make any difference to him? Don't let it make any difference to you."

"A thing like yesterday, it's humiliating. I can't just let it go without at least trying to separate myself from it."

I patted him on the back. "Relax, Joe," I said. "You're separated."

"You understand that there's nothing I can do about him."

"That was obvious from the first. There's nothing anybody could do."

"Thanks," he said. We were still on the doorstep. "Do you have to hang on out here to keep an eye on that guy who's working on your window or could I maybe come in and talk a little while?"

It could have been that he had nothing on his mind beyond seeking a sympathetic ear into which he could pour the problems of coping with the old bastard's senility. There was something in his manner, however, that said coming over to apologize for the old man might have been no more than a convenient pretext for paying me a visit that had some other purpose.

"The place is a wreck," I said. "But if you can stand it."

He could stand it. He waited for no further discussion. Before I had finished saying even that much, he was inside. I followed him in and shut the door behind us. He stood in the hall goggling at the relatively minor wreckage on display out there.

"Christ!" he said. "What happened?"

"Burglar last night. He ripped the whole place apart."

"Yeah. I can see."

"You haven't seen anything yet."

I guided him along the sort of trail I'd worked out between the front door and the living room. At the door to the living room he again invoked the Son of God.

"See what I mean," I said, settling him on a bar stool. Since they were all wood with no upholstery, they had seats that could be sat on.

"I've never seen anything like this," he said. "It looks like he was digging for buried treasure."

"He was interrupted before he got around to digging up the garden," I said.

"Interrupted? All this? It would have taken the whole night."

To this kind of talk I didn't have to give my undivided attention. I picked up again on sorting out the papers, but promptly thought better of it. I suppose when it comes to stalling I am never at a loss for finding ways. I offered my visitor a drink.

"You'll have one with me."

"I never let a man drink alone," I said. "What'll it be?"

"What have you got, or maybe it's what did your burglar leave you?"

"Everything and it's not only the liquor. So far I can't find that he took anything."

"How can you tell in all this mess?"

"I can't. One of the reasons I'm breaking my ass to get organized on it."

He asked for scotch and I took my usual. He was silent while I was pouring them. When he took the first drag on his, it was like a man fortifying himself to speak.

"Lans and you," he said. "You weren't really friends."

"Statement or question?"

"Something of both. I'm pretty sure, but it was hard to know with Lans. The way he talked he was great buddies with everyone. I was thinking you might tell me I'm right."

"We weren't enemies. We saw each other pretty often at the club, always pleasant and friendly."

"But never bosom buddies."

"No, never bosom buddies."

"Obviously. Anybody could see that, anybody but my father. My father and Lans. Lans liked to kid himself that everyone loved him like a brother. My old man never could see through it because he never could see Lans for the louse that he was. My beloved cousin was a phony—a sneak, a liar, and a cheat. He was always coming at you with the big buddy act, and behind it he was malicious all the way through. He'd do a man dirty for nothing more than the kick of it. A man would have to be a fool or my father not to be aware of it, and you're no fool."

"On the sound of that," I said, "he was a man who made enemies."

"I don't know. I think it was more that people sensed the phony in him and never let him get close enough to give him a chance to shaft them. The ones who did were stupid. I can see them crawling away just hurt and bewildered or else never knowing what hit them —at least not knowing where it came from because Lans would be right there with the big smile and the phony sympathy. If he had any friends who weren't idiots, they'd have to be masochist types that kept coming back for more."

"His killer doesn't fit into any of your categories," I said.

"His killing?" McLeod said, with the air of a man who was tossing off the self-evident. "That was professional. On a good guess it was done by a guy who didn't even know him, just a pro who had his orders and delivered according to specifications."

"What makes you think that?" I asked.

It was no less self-evident to me than his tone indicated it would be to him, but I had marked advantages over him. I'd had far more experience with looking at murder than he could have had. It seemed likely that prior to his cousin's killing he would have had none. Also I had been briefed by Inspector Schmidt. I was asking the question only out of curiosity about how it would look to someone who was not so much an insider.

He could have been reading my thoughts.

"Oh, come on," he said. "You were at the funeral. How dull do you think I am? You saw the flowers. Who sends flowers like that? Anyhow they were there. I don't know who the fat guy is, but just looking at him and the lugs he had with him, anyone could tell. And Smiley Donohue—I knew him right off. For me that was just from seeing newspaper pictures. If I could recognize them, don't tell me you couldn't, or at least your cop friends must have told you. The one you were with, riding out to the cemetery, I figured that was Inspector Schmidt. You weren't out there mourning Lans. You were keeping an eye on those guys."

"The inspector was keeping an eye on them," I said. "I just go along for the ride."

"Yes," he said, "I know. The old man's wrong on that, too, just as he's wrong on you and Lans being such great buddies. You aren't a detective. It's the inspector, and you just write about him. You make that perfectly clear in your books."

He had opened it up. There was no reason why I shouldn't ask some questions. I was curious and the questions I had in mind were ones I was certain the inspector would have wanted asked.

"Tell me something," I said. "Did you have any idea that your cousin was mixed up in any gang stuff or was the funeral a complete surprise to you?"

"It was more than a surprise, George. It was a blow."

I hadn't suggested that he call me George but, since he had asked me to call him Joe, I could suppose that it followed. It was unimportant and I had a question I wanted to get in quickly.

"Why a blow? The way you seem to have felt about your cousin Lans . . ."

"As my father keeps telling me, blood is thicker than water. I could ask him what's so good about thicker, but it wouldn't be any use."

"Let me understand you," I said. "You already had so low an opinion of your cousin that low or lower can't make any difference.

So was it your father you were concerned about? Was it a blow to you that your father was being confronted with it and would be upset?"

"Daddy upset? George, you don't know my father. There's only one thing that can ever upset him, or maybe it's two—if he's contradicted by anyone about anything or if he is not obeyed. His nephew Lans was golden boy, all the perfections rolled into one, and that was it. Fact, argument, evidence, proof to the contrary had no effect. Daddy had passed judgment. Nothing ever puts the smallest dent in that."

"What's his explanation for the flowers and the big gang turnout?" I asked.

All through this talk I was sorting papers. I was not making rapid progress with it and, when I came to deal with them finally, I found several sheets sorted wrong, but I didn't miss out on seeing anything that could have been of any possible interest to Inspector Schmidt.

Meanwhile McLeod had found a way of being helpful. The books strewn all over had been dropped every which way. Some had fallen open and face down with some of the pages mauled. He was picking books up, smoothing pages, closing them carefully, and stacking them neatly. He was making no attempt to shelve them. I was covering the shelves with my sorting of the papers.

Books that had been mistreated, however, he was rescuing from suffering further damage. I had watched him do it for a moment or two and I had satisfied myself that he was a man who treated books lovingly. He dealt with two or three books while he thought about my question.

"The flowers," he said. "Some idiot of a florist delivered them to the wrong church. Gangsters in attendance? Who says they are gangsters? If they came to the funeral, they must have been Lansing's friends, and if they were Lansing's friends, they aren't gangsters. Daddy says so and Daddy knows best. The police and the FBI don't agree with him? That doesn't prove anything but that the police and the FBI don't know their business, and that has been obvious anyhow. If they knew their business and did their job, poor Lansing would be alive today."

In the course of making this insane statement he had picked up a special volume. It was a book I most particularly treasured, first edition of the one novel that would head my list of books I'd want with me if ever I was marooned on a desert island. It is a book I love in any edition, but this was a first and rare to the extent of being virtually irreplaceable.

Much as I enjoyed owning it, it would have been an extravagance I would never have permitted myself if it had not come to me as a bequest from a much-loved friend. So, apart from everything else, I had with it that emotional involvement. Despite its age, it was in excellent condition. For its protection my late friend had commissioned from a master bookbinder a beautiful slipcase for it.

It had been dropped on a mound of the black horsehair stuff that had been pulled out of the sofa's slashed upholstery. My first thought was of thankfulness that it'd had a soft landing, but that was immediately followed by a chilling one. It had been in the hands of the most destructive of vandals. I reached out and took the book from McLeod.

Respecting my concern, he was silent while I inspected for damage. I could find none. Meanwhile I was telling him the reasons for my alarm. He was sympathetic.

I started to look around for the slipcase. Everything else was going to wait until I'd found that and had the book safely stowed inside it. McLeod asked what I was looking for. He wanted to know if he could help. Even as he was offering, however, I spotted it. It couldn't have been more in plain sight. It was sitting on top of another heap of the black upholstery stuffing. I reached out and retrieved it.

If I had seen the slipcase sooner, it would have reminded me of the book and I would have been on a hunt for it. In the general chaos, it was difficult to focus on any one thing even when it was right before your eyes. Everything was a dazzle of confusion. My whole apartment could have served as a lesson in camouflage.

The case was beautifully made. It was a close fit to the book but with just enough give so that the book slid in or out smoothly and easily. Now, when I tried to slip it in, it wouldn't go unless I forced it. I wasn't going to force it. The thing hadn't come through disaster as fortunately as I had hoped. There had been some damage either to the binding or to the case. I found a safe place on one of the bookshelves to set the book and ran my hand inside the case. I could feel the unevenness in the lining.

It had seemed like Inspector Schmidt's most far-out idea, but here it was—the paper concealed in the apartment and safely hidden. It was the one thing the burglar had wanted. For it he had ripped the whole place apart. He had come close. He had all but had it in his hands, and he had missed.

My first impulse, of course, was to rip the lining out of the slipcase and bring out whatever had been hidden there. I even got so far as bringing my pen knife out of my pocket. As I approached the edge of the lining with the blade, however, I had second thoughts. The case had miraculously escaped the depredations of the vandal. I couldn't bring myself to mess it up. It would have to wait. I would take it around to the artist who had made it and have him deal with it—take out whatever was hidden in it and put the case back to rights. I put my knife away and set the case on the shelf alongside the book.

I didn't return to sorting the papers. Now all that could wait. It was no longer a matter of Schmitty's concern, only of my convenience. I turned back to McLeod.

"All that you were telling me about your father," I said, "is that what he's been saying?"

"He's been saying nothing, but I know him. That's what he's thinking."

"Okay then, Joe, we're back to my first question. It was a blow to you. What made it a blow?"

"I'm going through every kind of hell, and until I do something about it, it will go on and on. I can't continue taking it. It's my old man."

"You've lost me," I said.

"We're McLeods. A wrong done to one McLeod is a wrong done to all of us. Lans is a McLeod because his mother was a McLeod. His death has to be avenged. An eye for an eye."

"That's pretty primitive."

"You're telling me. The old bastard's my father. I have to live with it."

"So?"

"So I get no peace till the murderer has been found and killed."

Perhaps I shouldn't have laughed. The guy was sweating, but control can go only so far.

"From the orders your father gave me after the funeral service," I said, "I thought I was the one picked for that duty."

"You were, George, but you disappointed him. He has you tabbed as a friend unworthy of wonderful, wonderful Lans. You won't push the villain into trying to escape so you can shoot him down like a rat."

"Nor will Inspector Schmidt," I said. "You can't ask it."

"I know I can't. The old man doesn't know it. He's never known anything he didn't want to know. He thinks he can ask it. No. Ask is the wrong word. My father doesn't ask. He demands. He thinks he can demand it, but he knows he won't be obeyed. It makes him impossible to live with."

"I'm sorry, Joe, but this is crazy. You must know it is. I can see how it's hell for you, but you must see that there's no way anyone can help you. More than that, I don't see how the gang involvement makes it any the worse for you."

"You don't understand. If it was just some guy and no gang connection, I could hope the police would get him. He'd stand trial and he'd go to prison. That wouldn't do for the old man. It wouldn't be the McLeod way—no eye for an eye. All the same, it would be manageable. I could find a way of handling it."

"How?"

"It would only take money. I hire another prisoner to murder him. The old man doesn't demand that I do it with my own hands, and he'll gladly come up with whatever it costs."

"You must be kidding."

"Come around to the house some time and spend a couple of hours with my father and you'll know I'm not kidding."

"You want me to believe that what is bugging you is that with a gang connection getting the murderer knocked off in jail will be impossible to arrange even with your old man's money?"

"Not exactly that. You know how it goes with these gang things, George. The police catch the man and the gang comes up with every kind of alibi witness. Even if he should come to trial, the gang lawyers get him off. There's going to be only one way I can deal with that."

"You can?"

"I'll need Inspector Schmidt's help."

"The inspector lets him try to escape and shoots him? No dice, Joe. Nobody has enough money to buy that, not you and not your father."

"No, of course not, and it wouldn't work anyhow. The gang types, they wouldn't try to run. Why should they? They know their gang boss will get them off."

"Then what?"

"Maybe you could do it yourself. If you knew from the inspector before he arrested the guy and you'd tip me off, I could get him before he's taken in."

"Murder him?"

"McLeods call it execution."

"No dice, Joe. You're out of your mind."

"I will be if I can't get the old man off my back."

"I wouldn't do it. If for no other reason, it's impossible because I would never do it to the inspector. Beyond that, nothing could ever persuade me to be party to a murder."

"How could I arrange to get in where he'd be kept after he's arrested? Nobody would have to be a party to that. I'd do it all on my own. You know, like Ruby and Oswald."

"Just to get your old man off your back you're prepared to go to prison for murder?"

"I wouldn't go to prison."

"Don't kid yourself, son."

"My father has the money for the lawyers it needs and for the psychiatrists it needs. Temporary insanity—it runs in the family."

"I'm going to have to tell Inspector Schmidt about this conversation. I would have warned you of that if I could have had any idea that it would take this turn. To be honest with you, it never occurred to me. It's too crazy."

"That's all right, George. I was just going to ask you. If you could just get me a meeting with the inspector, I could put it up to him directly."

"You never needed anyone to arrange that," I said. "You were on his agenda anyhow. He'll be talking to everyone who knew your cousin. Part of what he needs in these things is everything he can learn about the victim."

"The victim," McLeod said. "The way things are right now, it isn't Lans. It's me."

CHAPTER 6

Once I had assured him that there was no chance that he wouldn't have his shot at talking to Inspector Schmidt, even though I made it clear that I was not going to suggest it to the inspector, much less arrange it for him, he seemed to be satisfied. He had me wondering whether he could be that much confident of his persuasive powers or even of the powers of persuasion of the McLeod money or if even within the all-too-extensive boundaries of his insane notions of the possible he recognized that making his pitch to the inspector would be the ultimate of what he could do. Either way, he appeared to be content to settle for that much, just an opportunity to put his case to Inspector Schmidt.

It was obvious that offering apologies for Daddy's behavior had been no more than a pretext. The object of his visit, I was now convinced, had been to make this fantastic request. It struck me as the more fantastic because in all other respects he came on as a normal human being—normal, in fact, to the point of being boring. I could only think that the pressures of coping with so difficult a father had put a warp in his values.

He looked at his watch.

"Damn," he said. "I've got to run. If I'm away any longer, the old man will blow his top. He'll refuse to believe I've just been over here. He'll be thinking I've been slipping my leash."

I saw him to the door. The work on the window bars was coming along fast. While I was looking at it, the upholsterer turned up. I left him to inspect the damage and phoned the inspector. I couldn't get through to him. He was closeted with the Police Commissioner.

If a session of that sort is ever interrupted, it's never going to be just so he can take a call from George Bagby. I left word, asking that he call me.

The upholsterer was moaning and mumbling. When I came away from the phone, he lifted it to an articulate level. What he was saying related only to the wrecker who had worked his beautiful upholstery over. It might have been mine by rights of ownership. It had been his by rights of creation. He was mourning it. He was saying nothing that I had myself not been thinking and saying even though I had been drawing on a broader vocabulary of epithets. He was a considerable time unburdening himself of all that before he could come around to telling me that he had to agree that the damage to chairs and sofa was irreparable. Only the frames could be salvaged.

He had come in his truck and was prepared to cart the furniture off to his shop. I would have to come around to choose the new covering material, but meanwhile he could make a start on the job. There was much to do before he would reach the covering stage. He carried the chair frames out to the truck and I gave him a hand with the sofa.

As I came back into the apartment the phone was ringing. It was the inspector.

"You called me," he said. "Can I hope you found something?"

"Something," I said. "You know, Schmitty, I've been looking because you said I should. You thought it just might be worth doing. I didn't believe it for a minute, but I was going along—only that, just going along. But there is something. The bastard had it in his hands and he missed it."

The inspector broke in on me. "Okay," he said. "What is it?"

"I don't know. It's hidden in the slipcase of a book. It looks as though the lining of the case was loosened, the thing was slipped under the lining, and the lining pasted down again."

"You've left it that way? You haven't lifted the lining?"

"It's securely pasted down. I don't know whether it can be lifted without damaging it. I know I couldn't do it without messing it up. I want to take it to the man who made it and see what he can do with it. The guy's an artist. He has the right tools and the right skills. If anyone can do it without damaging the case, he will."

"What's a slipcase?"

"It's like a box. It's made to just fit a valuable book. It's something of a protection."

"Don't touch it and don't do anything about it. Just wait for me. I'll be right over to look at it. I was coming over anyway."

I knew I wasn't going to have long to wait, and it wasn't long. When the inspector moves, he moves fast, and he'd said he was on his way. Within minutes he was out in front, inspecting the job being done on my window bars. The man had almost finished. The inspector looked me over.

"We're going visiting. You'll want to do a little cleanup on yourself," he said.

"Whom do we visit?"

"Mrs. Mallory, Celia Mallory. You saw her in the church. She was there with her husband, John."

"One of the couples. Doing them all and starting with her?"

"All if we have to. She just may tell us which way to go."

"What's about her particularly?"

"The boys I had talk to her have the impression she has something she wants to spill. I'll tell you about it, but now let's see this box or case or whatever it is."

I led the inspector to the bookshelf. Schmitty slipped his hand inside the case and felt the lining surface.

"Nice," he said. "Very nice. It feels like a small envelope. It bulks a bit thick, but for an envelope that small it's likely that whatever is in it is folded several times over. I don't have to ask you if maybe you didn't put it there yourself some time and then let it slip your mind."

"Since you don't have to, then don't ask it," I said. "I'd hate to think you could imagine I'd be such an idiot."

"The brightest people can be absentminded, but it isn't possible that finding it wouldn't have reminded you. There's another thing though. Could it have been there all the time? Could it have been put there by the previous owner? You never had occasion to look inside before. So you wouldn't have noticed."

"Not possible."

"Why not? It's an old book. You weren't even around yet when it was new. You got it secondhand or rather after a whole slew of other people had owned it."

I told him how it had come to me.

"With the box?" he asked. "The box is a lot newer than the book."

"Yes. The box was made for it while it belonged to the man who left it to me."

"Couldn't he have put the envelope in there?"

"No. The case was made to fit the book. The book slid in and out of it easily. I didn't find the thing just by looking at the case. I found the book lying face down and open, out of the case. It's a rare book. It's valuable and, apart from that, it means a lot to me. I was afraid it might have been damaged."

"You haven't done anything about any of the other books. They look like they're lying just the way the guy dumped them."

"That's right. I haven't started on the books . . ."

I was about to say I'd been working on the papers instead, but I saw that the inspector's gaze had shifted to the books McLeod had stacked neatly. I broke off to explain that.

"Joe McLeod did those. I was on the papers and we were talking."

"Who?"

It was more an exclamation than a question.

"Josiah McLeod, Jr."

"He was here?"

"He came to apologize for his old man. At least that's what he said he came for. He's going crazy, if he hasn't already gone. I have to tell you about him."

"You sure do, if only because he's his father's son."

"About the book and the slipcase," I said. "McLeod was picking up books and closing them and stacking them. He picked up this one. When I saw him with it, I took it out of his hand. I was afraid it had been damaged. When I saw it was all right, I started looking for the case because I wanted to put it into the case and up on a shelf where it would be out of harm's way. The case was right out in plain sight, but in all the mess, I just hadn't been seeing it."

"You said the book always slipped in and out of the case easily."

"Yes. Now when I tried to slip it in, it wouldn't go. It wasn't the easy fit anymore. That's how I came to find the bulge under the lining."

Schmitty picked up the book and the slipcase. He was about to try the fit.

"Don't force it. I'd rather it wasn't damaged."

He went at it gently and carefully. As soon as he met resistance, he pulled the book out.

"No need to try," he said. "No question. It's too tight."

I noticed what seemed to be a dark smudge on the book's binding. Thinking that even if it hadn't suffered other damage, it had been soiled, I took it from the inspector's hand. It wasn't a smudge. It was just some wisps of the upholstery stuffing out of the sofa clinging to the binding. I picked them off.

"This stuff," I said, holding up the black fibers, "this is what saved it. It didn't hit the floor. It landed soft on a pile of this stuffing material."

The inspector showed little interest in that. "Since you've owned the book," he said, "you've had it out of the case and back in?"

"Yes. Many times."

"Always easy?"

"Smooth as butter."

"When did you last have it out?"

"Gosh, Schmitty, I don't know."

"Not recently?"

"A month ago. Two months. Something like that. I'd say not more than two months."

I explained to him that somewhere in the disordered mess there was another copy of the same book. That was one I'd owned ever since college when I first fell in love with the book. It was a modern edition that might bring ten bucks and probably less from a secondhand dealer. It was a book I had been rereading regularly ever since my first reading of it.

"I read it straight through about every five years," I said. "I don't read it in this rare edition. For reading I have my old copy. In addition to going through it from beginning to end that way, I am always reading in it. That's just a couple of pages a time, but it's three or four times a week."

"Like my grandfather used to read the Bible," the inspector said.

"I don't think the Bible made your grandfather laugh," I said. "This is a beautiful and wonderfully funny book."

"Nothing ever made my grandfather laugh," Schmitty said. "So you look into it almost every day or every other day, but not this copy. When do you have this one out?"

I explained that there were times when something might strike me as a bit odd in one passage or another. Then I'd want to compare with my first edition to see if there had been a change in the text.

"That's it mostly," I said. "Other times it will be that a book collector has come around and we're talking books. I'll bring it out for him to look at."

"Do many people know that you're always reading this book or anyhow little pieces of it? Does anybody know?"

I shrugged. "A lot of people must know," I said. "Any time I'm talking books with anyone, I'm likely to take off on it and say I'm reading in it almost every day."

"Did Monroe know?"

"He might have. I can't remember ever talking books with him, but around the club he might have heard me talking to some other guy or heard someone kidding me about being hooked on it. I'd have no way of knowing."

"Had he ever been here? Visiting you? To a party?"

"No, but I'm in the phone book, and now I know anyone could have come in or out through the kitchen window. It's damned uncomfortable to think it was used by someone I knew. Whatever it is in there was hidden for me to find it. It must have been done by somebody who had reason to believe that in the ordinary course of events it would be no more than a day or two before I would come on it. That's someone who knew about my addiction. He just didn't know I had the other copy and that I wouldn't be constantly leafing through this one. That was a natural mistake."

"If you're upset because you're thinking you've been betrayed by a friend, I can tell you one thing—he was no friend."

"No question of that," I said.

I was thinking that Schmitty was laboring the self-evident. A man who has invaded your home secretly to tamper with one of your prized possessions has by that act alone proved himself no friend. As I should have known, however, the inspector was thinking in terms more relevant.

"You never considered Monroe a friend," he said.

"It had to be Monroe?"

"Or someone connected with him. Anything else gets you into unbelievable coincidence."

I had to agree. It happens. A man knows that someone is out to kill him. He can think of only one way to protect himself. He writes a letter addressed to the police. In it he points them to his murderer in the event that he should be murdered. He deposits the letter with someone he can trust, instructing that if anything happens to him, the letter is to go to the police.

To complete his move, he then lets his enemy know what he's done in the hope that the man will decide to forget it since he will realize that he cannot get away with it. I put this picture of the thing to the inspector.

"It looks that way, doesn't it?" Schmitty said.

"But why would I be picked for it? That's what baffles me."

"You were his detective friend, kid," Schmitty said.

"Only in the mind of one crazy old man."

"Yes. Monroe probably did know better, but he would have figured that through your connection with me, you had access that other people wouldn't have. The world is full of guys like that. They hate to go about things like everyone else. They always want to have some privileged approach. It doesn't even have to give them any kind of an edge. If it gives them the feeling of being privileged, that's enough. I see Lansing Monroe as one of those guys. Even in death he would like the idea of having an inside track."

"Listening to you," I said, "I could think you had known him."

"If you're a cop, you see his kind in wholesale lots."

"The whole thing falls into place," I said. "The killing was a gang job. With those babies his ploy wouldn't work. They knock him off and leave it to their attorneys and their influence to take care of any problems. Then the old man broadcasts that 'detective friend' nonsense. They probably know I'm no detective and that I'm not on the force, but they probably also know that I'm close to you."

Schmitty chuckled. "If they can't read," he said, "they'll know someone who does."

"Right," I said. "They'd been prepared to take their chances, but if there could be a cheaper way of handling it, why not? They know better than to believe the detective part of the old man's nonsense, but they'd have no reason to doubt the friend part and that would make me the most likely person to whom Monroe might have entrusted the letter. I might still have it since you hadn't yet made any move against them. It would have seemed to them it was worth a shot."

"It's nice," the inspector said. "It's even beautiful. I wish there could be a way of making it fit with the rest of what we have. Celia Mallory seems to be suggesting something far more personal."

"With a machine gun?"

"There are a lot of them around. They hang on the walls of family rooms in nice suburban houses. Guys brought them home as souvenirs from Vietnam, Korea, World War II."

"Revolvers they took off enemy prisoners, but machine guns?"

"Yup, Baggy. Even machine guns." He looked at his watch. "Clean up," he said. "I want to catch Mrs. Mallory before her husband comes home from the office."

"I'll have to pass this one up," I said.

I explained that I had to hang around to take delivery on the new mattresses.

"I'm putting a man on here for while you're out. He'll take the delivery for you."

"What for?" I asked. "We have the one thing they were after. All he'll be doing is protecting the wallpaper."

"Have you had your locks changed?"

"What for? It was the window not the door, and the window is being barred."

"When an intruder's had a lot of time in a place, it's smart not to take chances."

He explained that there were too many people who knew how to take impressions of locks and make keys to fit them. Until the locks had been changed the apartment was not going to be left empty at any time. He hit the phone and arranged for a locksmith to come in. Then he called precinct and had them send a man over.

I went into the bedroom to change. While I shaved and switched into something more presentable than grimy jeans and T-shirt, he stood in the doorway waiting.

"You were going to tell me what Junior came for," he said. "I'll swap that for Senior's performance of the day."

"The old man's been performing?"

"In a big way, but you first."

I repeated for him the talk I'd had with Joe McLeod. "The guy wasn't kidding," I said in conclusion. "He meant exactly what he said. He was serious."

"I don't doubt it," the inspector said. "This is one you can call deadly serious."

"I was thinking that maybe we might help the poor guy out," I said.

The inspector scowled. "None of that, Baggy," he said. "You don't have his old man on your back. No reason for you to go out of your mind."

"Help him commit murder?" I said. "Of course not. Just this. Suppose the letter, or whatever it is, gives you what you need to arrest someone and prove the killing on him, wouldn't it be possible to let it be known how the thing was found? You know, build his part in it up a little. Feed it that way to the papers. I'm thinking like headlines: 'Josiah McLeod, Jr., Uncovers Evidence to Convict Cousin's Killer.' It would just be so the old man would feel that Junior had recognized that blood is thicker than water and had done his vengeful duty as a properly barbaric McLeod."

"Not a chance," Schmitty said.

"What harm could it do?"

"What good could it do? Not a chance it would get the old bastard off Junior's back. A conviction isn't going to satisfy him. It is that good old eye for an eye or tooth for a tooth. Conviction's a slap on the wrist. Let me tell you what I heard from the Commissioner."

"About this? About the murder of the Monroe twerp?"

"The murder of the finest man that ever lived," Schmitty said.

He broke off to push me toward his car. The man had come from precinct and we stopped long enough to tell him about the mattress delivery. Out in the street there was a further small delay. The window had just been finished. I stopped to write the man a check.

"The murder of the finest man who ever lived?" I said as the inspector pulled away from the curb.

"The exact words as quoted by the Commissioner from what the Mayor had quoted from Josiah McLeod, Sr. More than that, Monroe was a McLeod. He was the son of old Josiah's dear dead sister, and no McLeod would ever rest until Lansing Monroe had been suitably revenged."

"What did he expect the Mayor to do about it?"

"Give the orders. The murderer was to be shot down while attempting to escape. He regretted the fact that we don't use machine guns, but he's not an unreasonable man. He's ready to concede that much. Police revolvers will do as long as we shoot and shoot to kill and don't miss."

"He got through to the Mayor with that garbage?"

"Josiah McLeod, Sr., gets through. His campaign contributions guarantee him that much."

"That the police will pull off a murder for him?"

"That," the inspector said, "had better not happen."

"Does he really think that his campaign contributions could buy him that?"

"I wish I could say he couldn't buy it."

"Everybody knows that politicians are money-hungry," I said, "but I just can't believe the Mayor's been telling the Commissioner to pass that kind of an order on to you."

"No," the inspector said, "not that. With the kind of money McLeod can dangle, it wouldn't have been impossible for him to get to some cop. It's happened too many times. A guy has a perfect record. He's the model cop. Then he gets the offer and the money is just too big. McLeod just might have brought it off, but he's over-reached himself. Going to the Mayor with it, he's killed it."

"Why can't he still find himself that vulnerable cop?"

"He'll have to find a crazy one. The Commissioner had me in to tell me that he's had orders from the Mayor. On this Monroe killing we go like as if we were disarmed. If any suspect is shot while re-sisting arrest or trying to escape, the officer who fires the shot will stand trial for Murder One with the Mayor himself supplying the evidence."

"And to hell with campaign contributions?"

Schmitty laughed. "The Mayor," he said, "has always been a good gambler. It's not like reelection will be coming up this year. He still has three to go. All right. Maybe it's only a year before he starts going after the campaign money. The odds are too good that old McLeod won't live another year."

I'd been too much interested in what he was telling me to have taken any notice of where he was driving. I was not unaware of the many high-speed narrow squeaks he negotiated as he threaded through the city traffic. Nothing has ever had me so much en-grossed that I have been able to ride along with him in happy igno-rance of the repeated brushes with death. This time, however, I had only the frisson of terror. I was keeping no track of the streets he was taking for our living dangerously. When I did get around to taking notice, we were careening along the Franklin D. Roosevelt Drive headed downtown. The Queensboro Bridge was behind us.

"This dame," I said. "Where does she live?"

"The Village."

I thought back to the couples I had seen at the funeral service. I had no memory of any of them that carried even the remotest sug-gestion of a Greenwich Village type. I remarked on it.

"Funny," I said. "The way I saw them, they all had the Fashiona-ble-Upper-East-Side look, like Sixties and Seventies east of the park and too with-it to be far east even there."

"How about West Tenth just off Fifth?"

"That's not the Village. That's Fashionable Lower Fifth Avenue."

The inspector sniffed. "Trouble with you, Baggy," he said, "is you read the society pages in the papers. It's been getting to you."

CHAPTER 7

In Tenth Street the inspector pulled up in front of one of the fine old houses. These are not the huge, ostentatious jobs that have been abandoned by their millionaire owners and are now headquarters of foundations or schools or consulates. These are survivors of the New York Henry James and Edith Wharton knew. Affluent people lived in them and lived tastefully and well. Although some have been divided into handsome apartments, others have remained intact, apart from the intrusion of modern kitchens, bathrooms, plumbing, electricity, and sometimes air conditioning.

People still live in them tastefully and well. With the assistance of modern appliances they can be run with fewer servants than in the old days. I have always thought of them as housing the city's most civilized way of life, therefore assuming that their occupants would inevitably be the town's most civilized citizens. That day my faith was shaken.

The door was opened to us by a stiffly starched black maid. It seemed impossible that in her crackling costume she should be able to do any work beyond opening a door. She might have been gotten up for a revival of some old drawing-room comedy.

The inspector introduced himself and said he would like to speak to Mrs. Mallory.

"I will see if madame is available, sir."

She sounded as though she had memorized her lines but was anything but comfortable with them. Leaving us on the doorstep with the door ajar, she made a loudly rustling ascent of the stairs.

She wasn't long. Madame was available. If we would just come along with her.

She led the way upstairs. The house had not been divided into apartments and there was every indication that these people were not land-poor. In every detail the place was everything it should have been. At every turn it spoke of money, but never stridently. It didn't shout. It spoke softly.

Celia Mallory received us in an upstairs sitting room. It was a beautiful room and I wondered how a woman who had it for her sitting could confront the world with Celia Mallory's look of sour discontent. I had noticed it at the funeral. I was remembering that I had pitied her husband. He hadn't looked pitiful, but I would have pitied anyone who had to live with this woman.

She welcomed us graciously, however. I might have said even warmly.

"Sit, gentlemen," she said. "Do sit. Since the police officers who called yesterday said they don't drink on duty, I have ordered tea. Or aren't you on duty, Inspector?"

"I am on duty," Schmitty said. "I hope you don't mind."

"Mind? I'm pleased you came now when we can have a nice talk. It would have been difficult later. My husband will interrupt."

"You knew Lansing Monroe well?"

"I knew him well. I knew him like a book."

"Would you like to begin by telling me what you had against him?"

"I had nothing against him. It was nothing to me. I couldn't have cared less. Judging is one thing, Inspector, and caring is another. Lansing Monroe was not a nice person. Not that he should have been murdered, Inspector. I am unalterably opposed to violence. Even if a murder is fully justified, it's unjustified."

I was dazzled by that last statement, trying to visualize how a witness who used the language with so flexible an attitude toward meaning would do on the stand.

"Not a nice person," the inspector said. Obviously, he hadn't come to hear what position Mrs. Mallory took on murder and he wouldn't have my fascination with her strange ways with language. "Could you be more definite?"

The expression on the lady's face which I had come to think might be a permanent fixture, abruptly changed. Now it was a look of gleeful spite. It was evident that she not only could be more definite but that she was looking forward to it eagerly. Since at that point the maid came in with the tea tray, the lady was able to prolong the joys of anticipation. She was evidently an observer of that age-old custom—you don't talk about anything before the servants. For some minutes, therefore, it was only the manipulation of silver tea service and thin china tea cups.

"How strong do you like your tea? Sugar? Milk? Do have a watercress sandwich. We have quite given up on cucumber. They will wax the skins. Repulsive! In the country where we can have them straight out of the garden, they're lovely. Here they're hopeless. Inspector, I should think you could do something about what they're doing to fruit and vegetables. It is a crime, after all."

"I'm Homicide, Mrs. Mallory," the inspector said.

"But nonetheless, Inspector, those waxed cucumbers are certainly lethal."

On the table alongside the inspector's chair there was a silver cigarette box. The inspector raised the lid. The box was well filled.

"So are cigarettes, Mrs. Mallory," he said, as he let the lid drop shut.

She laughed. "*Touché*, Inspector," she said. "You are a clever man."

Apart from the gleefully spiteful look which not even for a moment was leaving her face, she was being every inch the gracious if flitter-witted hostess. It lasted only till the cups and sandwiches had been passed. The lady then was quick to clear the decks. She was losing no more time.

"Thank you, Deborah," she said. "We shan't need you anymore. I am sure one of the gentlemen will pass the cakes for me when we are ready for them."

As soon as the maid had withdrawn and shut the door behind her, Mrs. Mallory let go.

"I cannot think well of a man who incurs responsibilities and just walks away from them. It's shameful. It's disgusting."

"What sort of responsibilities?"

"To the woman who was bearing his child. To his son and the mother of his son. Inspector, you can't think that's nice."

"He had a wife and a son and he abandoned them?"

"No, Inspector. That's not quite it."

The lady was talking and taking great enjoyment of it. It was obvious that it was not even some small measure of reticence that was leading her to keep things vague. Since she was having fun, she was prolonging the pleasure. The inspector moved to cut through the fog.

"What is 'quite it' then, Mrs. Mallory?"

"They were never married, Inspector, unless it was, as the phrase goes, in the eyes of God. It does seem to me, though, that God would want to avert His eyes from anything so tawdry. It didn't surprise me when I saw her in the church. After all, she's always been stupid, a besotted bitch. What did surprise me was that she had the sense or good taste or something not to be wearing black. I shall never forget the wedding. You should have seen her then, coming up the aisle—virginal white satin, much white veil, and already showing that tribal increase was on the way. Maternity bridal dress, Inspector. Can you believe it? The whole bit—bell, book, and scandal."

"You said they never were married."

"He wasn't. She had to find someone else to make an honest woman of her. I believe that's the accepted way of putting it. She didn't have to look far. She had that huge lunk, Eliot Griffiths, ready to hand. I've always thought they named him Eliot because they couldn't find any name that would come closer to idiot. Big Biceps Griffiths, the muscle-bound brain."

"Are you thinking, Mrs. Mallory, that any of this might have something to do with Monroe's murder?"

She found a way to postpone making an answer to that. She turned to me.

"Could I ask you to pass the cakes to the inspector, Mr. Bagby? And please help yourself. Or perhaps you'd like more sandwiches first."

I passed the cakes while she discoursed on them. This one was chocolate and the paler one was mocha. The others were hazelnut.

She was herself partial to the hazelnut. She was certain that we would find them subtly delicious.

"The chocolate and even the mocha are blatant by comparison."

Both Schmitty and I made quick choices. We hadn't come down to Tenth Street in quest of cake. Our hostess lingered over her choice, exploring aloud the relative merits of each kind, weighing the frankness of the one against the subtlety of tho other. Eventually she settled on the chocolate, and I hoped there might be some element of the symbolic in her choice and that she was about to be frank.

"My question, Mrs. Mallory," the inspector said.

"Yes, Inspector. I haven't forgotten. When I told you your understanding of the state of affairs—that's a most suitable way of putting it: state of affairs—wasn't quite it, I was expecting then that I would have to explain to you the aspect of this thing that would be worth your attention. I cannot believe that you care a fig about who sleeps with whom as long as it doesn't lead to murder."

"Then you're thinking it does?"

"Once I've set you right on the other aspect you haven't grasped," she said, "you will see at once that it did lead to murder."

She had gone only that far when her husband came into the room. Breaking off to introduce him to us, she busied herself with seeing to his discomfort.

"I'll ring for fresh tea, darling," she said.

Darling didn't want tea. He was going to make himself a drink.

"Darling, do you really think you should? Is it polite since our guests can't because they are on duty?"

"Go ahead, Mr. Mallory," Schmitty said. "We don't mind."

Even as he was thanking the inspector, his wife jumped on it. "But I do mind," she said. "I very much mind when guests in my house are forced to be more polite than my husband."

"Our house, my dear," Mallory said.

There was a neat little bar at the far side of the room. He went to it and made himself one of those martinis that gives the vermouth no more than a cool nod. He used a glass that held about a bucketful and, the way he filled it, he had to sip it clear of the rim before he could carry it away from the bar to join us at the tea table.

"My wife has been gossiping," he said. "I can't tell you, gentlemen, that anything of what she's been telling you is not true or even that it's a stretched truth; but if you haven't already recognized as much, you can take my word for it that it is all totally irrelevant. Lansing Monroe was mixed up in the drug traffic. My first thought, when I heard about him, was that it had been a simple robbery murder. He always carried ridiculously large amounts of cash on him, and the newspapers said there was no money on the body."

"Money," his wife said. "I told you from the beginning that didn't mean anything. Some policeman robbed the body when he found it."

"Celia!"

If the tea table hadn't been in the way, I'm sure he would have kicked her. He had to do with the shocked exclamation and an inclination of his head in Inspector Schmidt's direction.

"It's all right," Schmitty said. "We have to be realistic. I prefer not to think it, but anything can happen. Of course, it's not the only possibility. Move it back to before the body was found. A passing mugger comes on the body. He thinks it's a drunk conveniently placed for rolling. Finding that the man is dead won't stop him. He'll see the money is there for the taking. The dead man won't need it."

"Move it back earlier than that," Mallory said. "He's quarreling with a drug pusher. The quarrel is about money. The pusher kills him and collects his debt off Monroe's body."

The redoubtable Celia charged back in there, battling.

"Darling," she said, "you know that's absurd. After all, the ape was filthy rich." It struck me that sitting as she was surrounded by all her appurtenances of wealth, Celia Mallory could hardly be calling a man filthy rich unless he had been dripping it from every pore. "You know how he was always throwing money around," she went on. "How you can imagine Lansing Monroe quarreling with anyone about money is beyond me. He had more than he knew what to do with. All sorts of people were in to him for money all the time. People didn't even have to ask."

That was an opening. Inspector Schmidt is not the man ever to miss one.

"Except his son and the mother of his son?" he said.

"Women, Inspector," Mallory said. "My wife has been determined to dredge that up, but it's ancient history, a closed book. There were never any hard feelings. Pru Griffiths has everything she ever wanted."

His wife interrupted. "Pru," she said. "Her name is Prudence, Inspector. How's that for low comedy? Nothing could be funnier unless it was Chastity."

"It's the same with Eliot." Mallory was ignoring the interruption. "He always wanted her. Beyond anything else he wanted her. Even when it seemed as though he could never have a chance, he was always hanging around like a housebroken Labrador hoping for scraps from the table. It never bothered him that when he could have her, it was only as Lansing Monroe's leavings. If anything, he was humbly grateful to Monroe for having turned her loose. He was Monroe's most devoted friend. They were having Monroe over to their place all the time. They've been so buddy-buddy all along that people have been making jokes about how strange it is that they didn't have Monroe in their wedding. They say the only reason not was because they couldn't decide on which role—Eliot's best man or to give the bride away."

The lady heard her husband out but she did it with an exaggerated show of tried patience and with a contemptuous curl of the lip. Taking it up when he left off, she mimicked him.

"Men, Inspector," she said. "Because he's a man, he didn't know what he was doing, but my husband has just brought up the very thing I had been about to tell you when he came in. You see, when you think of a man abandoning his wife and child, you get a picture of a poor woman left destitute. It wasn't at all like that. She bounced right into Eliot's arms. He hadn't, hasn't, and never will have Monroe's kind of wealth—after all, who has?—but Griffiths does have more than enough income so that Prudence, who is no more prudent about money than she is about bedfellows, never needs to want for anything and she doesn't."

She went on and on and now nobody was interrupting her. Her husband had been intent on stopping her from opening any of this up. Once he realized that it had been opened up, he relaxed. It was surrender. She had said so much that it didn't matter if she said the rest. I could guess that he was hoping she might empty herself of it and he might then hear the last of it.

She explained that when she'd told the inspector that he had it not quite right, her "not quite" had included the thought that Lansing Monroe had not quite abandoned Prudence Griffiths.

"He walked out and he stayed away from her. He wasn't at the wedding. He had to be out of town that week. He'd left her with some money. Since she made the quick grab for the Griffiths lunk and it worked, she didn't need it to carry her through any in-between period. The silly bitch blew it on the wedding. It would have been nothing for Monroe to have flown back to New York for it. Any fool could know that his being away that week was simply a strategic retreat. He sent a grand wedding present."

Either Mrs. Mallory was just surmising or out of malicious interest she had all along been at great pains to keep herself informed. She never once put it that she thought or she guessed. She was offering everything as incontrovertible fact. The way she had it, for a couple of years Lansing Monroe had carefully steered clear of Prudence Griffiths. They would meet at parties where he would be buddy-buddy with the husband but coolly and distantly correct with the wife, busying himself with some other woman in the company or promoting a table for poker which would take him from all the women.

Otherwise during this period he never went to the Griffiths house. He would see Griffiths downtown where they would lunch together or meet for drinks.

"Just recently," she said, "all that changed. Instead of just being Eliot's best buddy, he became the friend of the family. He was in and out of their place all the time. Anyone could see what was happening."

"No one could see anything," Mallory said. "You've just let your imagination run away with you. You're seeing what you want to see. It isn't there."

"She's pretty and she's sexy and that's all you can see. Past that you see nothing even when it's right before your eyes."

What she saw was that Monroe had still wanted Prudence. He had never stopped wanting her even though the dread word marriage had made him pull away and keep himself at a careful distance. On her side Prudence had always wanted him, and nothing had ever changed that. Griffiths had merely been a convenience.

"Until recently," Mrs. Mallory said, "Monroe hadn't been trusting it. He was afraid the marriage wouldn't hold and where was he to find another besotted idiot on whom he could unload her? As time went on and he saw how well they were doing together, he had the gall and the dreadful taste to go sniffing around her and she responded all too enthusiastically. Can't you imagine her thinking? She was having the best of both possible worlds. Griffiths for stability and marital bliss, and wonderful, wonderful Lansing for the main event."

"Right before your eyes, dear?" Mallory said. "I hope you're not going to tell the inspector you were an eyewitness. It would embarrass me to have you testifying that you had been in bed with them."

"Pay no attention to my clown, Inspector. There are all the little things that never escape a woman," Mrs. Mallory said. "Lansing Monroe made the one fatal mistake. Griffiths had never taken offense at anything Monroe had done to him. He'd been humiliated. He'd been played dirty. He'd taken everything without resentment —even with gratitude. Monroe assumed there could be no such thing as pushing good buddy too far. That hungry dog who snaps up your table scraps gratefully—just reach down to take them away from him and he'll tear your arm off. The animal would never be able to understand that you weren't taking it all. You were just sharing it. I'm sure Prudence has enough for at least two."

"And that's it?" the inspector said.

"You're probably wondering at his gall in coming to the church," she said. "It didn't surprise me. Nothing Eliot Griffiths could do could ever surprise me, not if it's stupid enough."

With that she stopped. It was evident that she had run out of

words. Schmitty was quick to sense that he would be having no
more from her. He turned to her husband. Mallory had finished his
mammoth martini and was at the bar pouring himself another.
Coming away from the bar, he held up his refilled bucket.

"The little wife," he said, "is salt of the earth, Inspector. Salt in
large doses makes me thirsty."

"That's my husband's clever, clever way of telling you that I
drive him to drink, Inspector. It's never been a long drive."

Schmitty had no interest in the Mallory marital harmony or lack
thereof.

"You have something to add to what your wife's been telling
me?" he asked.

"Something to add," Mallory said, "and much to subtract. Maybe
there are things that only the girls can see. There are also things
that are visible only to us boys. I know Bosco Griffiths one helluva
lot better than my wife ever will. Part of that is the things that boys
know. Part is that I have known him for a long time, ever since we
were at school together. Part of it is because she has never given
knowing him a chance because she's afraid of him. I'm not afraid of
him."

"That's telling me about Mrs. Mallory and yourself, not much
about Griffiths."

"Bosco? Yes. The dog and the table scraps. That's a brilliant
analogy, but the dog will tear your arm off. He won't go get himself
a machine gun and put a line of perforations across your belly. If
Bosco ever kills a man, he'll beat him to death with his bare fists or
he'll grab him by the throat and squeeze the life out of him. So my
good wife has just been wasting your time. Bosco Griffiths didn't
kill Lans Monroe. It's as simple as that. The way Lans was murdered could never be Bosco's style."

Celia Mallory jumped on that. "Absurd," she said. "Everyone
knows he's stronger than anybody. He could have been Griffiths the
Great, the circus strong man. There have been too many parties
where his contribution to the entertainment was picking people up
with one hand and holding them over his head or tearing telephone
books in two with his bare hands. You could follow his trail around
town by picking up a spoor of torn phone books. Even he isn't so

stupid that he would do a murder in what you call his style, as though it was some kind of work of art. There are people who do it for hire."

Mallory laughed. "Bosco? For him it would have to be in a moment of blind rage. Bosco can explode. He can't smolder. It would be instantaneous or nothing. A premeditated job—all that thinking that he can't do it his way and get away with it. That's out right there. If he did it, it would be without thinking. You want to have him rationalizing himself away from the quick impulse but holding it long enough for finding a killer, hiring him, setting the thing up. That would be a long-time-developing premeditated job. You can't have it both ways. You say he's dumb as shit."

"I don't use that kind of language and I'd prefer that you didn't, at least not at the tea table."

"I'm not at the tea table. I'm slurping a martini. Anyhow, you can't have it both ways. You're always saying he's an idiot. There's no argument there, but premeditated murder? How are you going to have premeditation where there is nothing to meditate with?"

CHAPTER 8

Before saying anything more that was at all germane, Mallory took time out to expand on the gentlemanly code he would have preferred to follow.

"I don't like gossip, Inspector. I would have chosen to have no part in it, but my good wife has left me no choice. What I must now tell you I consider to be private and humiliating. It will be humiliating to Bosco Griffiths that it has been made known. It's humiliating to me to be the one to talk about it. I shall try to tell myself that it was my obligation, my citizen's obligation to law and order, but I cannot put from me the recognition that the only reason why you should need to be told any of it is because my wife has planted in your mind ideas that must be adjusted. I cannot say that what she has been telling you is divorced from the truth. It is the truth, but seen, as it were, through a distorting lens."

It might have been a consciousness of the great weight of what he was going to say that made him find himself so pompous a way of saying it. It seemed to me, however, that at least some of the pomposity was martini engendered.

"The relationship between Bosco and Lans," he said, "was never anything I could have called friendship. There was nothing man-to-man about it ever. It was a dog-and-man relationship. You could describe what passed between them as the pat on the head and the wag of the tail. If Lans Monroe spit in Bosco Griffiths' eye, Bosco would fawn on him in gratitude for washing a cinder out of it. There's no way, Inspector, that can be equated with murder."

"Worms turn," Mrs. Mallory said.

"Good, old, faithful Fido doesn't," Mallory told her before returning to the inspector. "You might find that too vaporous," he said, "but there is also what we might call the golden-egg syndrome. Bosco is not a poor man, but there is a yawning gap between not poor and filthy rich. Lans was filthy rich, and Lans was at once generous and grasping. I will ask you to remember both of those. I shall be exploring them for you."

He began his exploration with the Griffiths' finances. Griffiths, he said, was well off. He had a good income; even very good. As a single man with no dependants he'd had no problems.

"Of course," he said, "he was in love with a most expensive woman; but as long as she wasn't his, she couldn't cost him too much. After all, candy and flowers—even if you go all out with those, and he did—they aren't any big bite."

The picture of the church as it had been, snowed under with flowers, rose in my mind, but I shoved it away. Griffiths, I told myself, hadn't been providing for the lady's funeral.

"But married," Mallory said, "and to that wife, was another story. She had to be kept in the manner to which Monroe had accustomed her. It could never occur to Bosco that he might do less. She didn't move into his little bachelor apartment. He moved into her penthouse, and the jump in rent was only the beginning. That was a temporary arrangement until she would find a town house that would suit her. He was going to have to buy her that. At today's market and today's mortgage rates that alone would bring him to the brink."

Mallory went into extensive detail. The lady was a dedicated shopper. The household bills and the bills for her clothes were staggering. What she considered was necessary for the child was commensurate. Also, she was not selfish. In buying for her husband she was equally lavish in the expenditure of her husband's money.

"That Bosco has all these bills to pay," Mallory said, "counts for nothing. That's taken for granted. Those are just the dull, routine necessities. What husband doesn't provide those? She expects gifts."

Those, he explained, had to be jewelry. She had the jewelry Lansing Monroe had given her and now Griffiths had to do more of the same.

"Much more," Mallory said, "because Lans wasn't even her husband. It doesn't have to be Cartier. She makes do with Winston or Van Cleef and Arpels. Birthday, Christmas, wedding anniversary. And how do you feel about irony, Inspector? Mother's Day."

"He does all that, even Mother's Day?" Schmitty asked.

"Bosco, Inspector, has never been much of a brain and he's besotted with the woman. No need to go on and on about it. The one who's hurt the worst by Lansing Monroe's death is Eliot Griffiths. It's not going to be a year before he'll be wiped out."

"You're saying Monroe was keeping him afloat? Loans the estate will be calling in?"

"No. That would be immediate ruin. There are no loans. I'm sure of that. There were a lot of little things that helped in a small way—the couple of cases of a good wine, the tins of caviar, tickets to the top hit plays, that sort of thing."

For a moment I was bemused with the thought of a way of life in which such items rated as trifles. I forced myself to forget that and keep my eye on the ball. Monroe had been keeping Griffiths afloat with market tips.

"Every time they lunched together downtown it was a market killing for Bosco. If he had been in a position to use any of those profits toward building up his capital—even though it's not been all that long, only since Monroe dumped the broad for Bosco to grab her on the bounce—Bosco would be in an invulnerable financial position by now. But all it could do for him was just keep him afloat. It's been going out as fast as it could come in. Now it won't be coming in anymore, and he has no way of stopping its going out. The poor guy's down the drain, and nobody can tell me he did that to himself."

Inspector Schmidt summed it up. "In brief then," he said, "he didn't kill Lansing Monroe because Monroe had him bought and paid for in a deal that included everything including the lady's favors?"

"If you want to look at it that way," Mallory said.

"What other way can you suggest?"

"There's the Fido bit. I sincerely believe that even without any financial factor it would have happened. I know Bosco and I knew

Lans. I suppose one might need to have known both of them well to be able to believe it. Bosco was that much at Lans's feet, and Lans would have done it just for the fun of having him there. It was his style with Bosco—to fondle with one hand and kick with the other."

"Kicking, my darling, is done with the foot," Mrs. Mallory said.

"I didn't know that, darling. Shall I learn it by practicing on you?"

"That will be the day."

Inspector Schmidt chose that moment for us to pull out of there. I know of no variety of murder that on one occasion or another the inspector has not confronted and investigated. A relatively common variety is murder at the family hearth. A lesser police officer might have had some concern at leaving the Mallory pair in that embattled state, but Schmitty dismissed it. He said it was of no consequence.

"Those two," he said, "aren't going to do anything. They know too many words. It's the ones who run out of words who go violent. Neither of them, while he still has something to say, is going to knock off a listener, and neither of them is ever going to run out of zingers they can throw at each other."

He had a point. These were people who never could be reduced to speechless fury. Their fury would always be anything but.

"I'm wondering," I said. "It seems to me you left some big questions unanswered."

The inspector corrected me. "Not unanswered," he said. "I left them unasked. What did you want me to ask?"

"What did Monroe do to make himself so damn rich?"

"Don't you know? You knew him."

"Yes, but not well. I never thought about it. I guess I never had occasion to think about it. For instance, I never noticed that he went around carrying any great sums in cash. If anyone had asked me, I would have said he was loaded. But as loaded as they indicate? Not many people are."

"If he gave Griffiths market tips that never missed, a broker wouldn't be a bad guess."

"One angle," I said, "but there was another."

"Involved with drugs," the inspector said.

"There's big money there. You didn't follow up on it."

"Where does a drug dealer get his steady supply of sure-fire inside market information? Why does a guy with access to that kind of information go in for drug dealing? He has this better way of making the big bucks. It's legal and nobody is going to go after him with a machine gun."

"Exactly. So why did you just let it lay?"

The inspector shrugged. "I'll go other places for those answers," he said. "If I don't get them elsewhere, I can go back to Mallory. I'd rather hit him for it when he's sober."

"Sober enough to know his hand from his foot?"

"At least that."

We had been sitting parked in front of the Mallory house. The inspector looked at his watch. I didn't have to look at mine. I knew it was time for a drink and dinner. Schmitty agreed to dinner.

"My drink will depend on when we can see your bookbinder."

"This evening? He shut up shop hours ago."

"Couldn't you reach him at home?"

"I suppose I could to make an appointment."

"If it can be right now, I'll drink with you. If it has to wait till after dinner, you'll drink alone."

"How can I ask him to do it after hours?"

"Urgent police business."

"If it's urgent, why didn't we go to him when you first saw it?"

Schmitty grinned. "I suppose we can't tell him we couldn't get to him earlier because we wanted to visit a lady when her husband wouldn't be home. Does he have to know we didn't just find it?"

"The things I do for you," I said.

"In the interests of justice, Baggy."

He picked up his car phone. I gave him the man's name and the address of the shop. He got through to the headquarters' switchboard and had them look up the phone number.

Although it was after hours and the shop was closed, there was no problem about reaching him. The man lived over his shop. I reminded him of the slipcase he had made for my dead friend. He didn't quite remember this particular job but he was certain he would recognize it when he would see it. My friend had been a good customer. Over a period of years he had brought the man a lot of work.

"What's happened to it?" he asked.

The tone made it an accusation. The words could have been: "What terrible thing have you done to it?"

I told him I'd had a burglar who had tampered with it.

"I'd like to have it put right," I said. "I think it will have to be relined. I would rather not have anyone else touching it."

"Can you bring it right over?"

"I can, but do you want to be bothered tonight?"

The question drew me a kick on the ankle from Inspector Schmidt. The good man did want to be bothered. It was as though he'd had bad news of one of his children and couldn't wait to see for himself. I hung up.

"He says to come right over."

"Small thanks to you, Mr. Bagby."

"It was the polite thing to say."

"One of these days, after I'm retired, you can teach me manners."

"We could have done this before we went to see Mrs. Mallory. You wanted to hear from both of them anyhow."

"But we wouldn't have been in time for tea," Schmitty said.

I was feeling more than a little annoyed with the inspector and very much baffled by what I could see only as his confused priorities. It seemed to me that in his handling of this case he was simultaneously dashing off in all directions. More than that, he seemed to be extraordinarily casual about it.

In the shop, with the bookbinder examining the slipcase, I began to feel very much abused. The man was looking at me with dark suspicion.

"A burglar didn't do this," he said.

"No," I said. "That thing in under there is what he was looking for and he missed it."

"He missed it because you hid it here. Couldn't you find any other place to hide it?"

He was ticketing me for an unappreciative savage with no right to own anything as beautiful as his slipcase, and even though he wasn't putting it into just those words, he was making no secret of his anger and contempt.

"I didn't," I tried to explain. "Someone else sneaked into my apartment and did that. I didn't know the thing was there till I had the burglar. He messed up the whole place. I discovered it when I was trying to put things back where they belong."

His look told me he didn't believe a word of it.

"It'll be easy to lift the lining and get that thing out of there and then paste the lining back down again. It's just the same as what was done in putting the thing in there, and you did that very neatly."

"I didn't," I said again. "And I have no intention of trying. I'd like you to do it."

"There's one difference," he said, again disregarding my denial. "Forcing that thing in there has stretched the lining paper and there's no way of shrinking the paper back again. The case will have to be relined. I'll do that." I started to thank him for taking it on, but he gave me no time to speak. "If it was just opening the lining, removing that thing of yours, and pasting the lining back, I don't mind telling you, mister, I wouldn't touch it. You come around here with a policeman and want me to handle it for you." He turned to Schmitty. "I assure you, Inspector Schmidt, I am not helping him to fool you into believing that he couldn't have done it. It's easy. Anyone could do it."

"I know that, sir," the inspector said. "His story is hard to believe, but it happens to be true. He won't let anyone else touch it, not because he wants to fool anyone but because he doesn't want it handled by anyone who might spoil it. He's a writer. If he was making up a story, he'd make it more believable. It's unbelievable only because it's true."

But nothing was changing the good old man's ideas. He was still glaring at me.

"I don't know," he said. "If he didn't do it himself, he let somebody else do it and that's not much better."

"You can take my word for it," Schmitty said. "It won't happen again. Meanwhile don't touch it till I get back. I'm only going out to my car. I'll be back in a minute."

"You don't have to feed the meter. That's only till six o'clock."

The inspector didn't stop to say he never fed parking meters whether before six or after. He just took off.

"He really a cop?" the old man asked.

"Inspector Schmidt. He's Chief of Homicide."

"Homicide. So he knows about people who kill people. He don't know about the kind of people I see all the time. They're murderers, too. They murder beautiful books. If he'd listen to me, I could tell him a thing or two."

The inspector returned with a small kit he'd brought from the car. The old man eyed it suspiciously. Schmitty explained.

"What I have here," he said, "is for bringing up fingerprints. Just open the lining so I can get at that thing tucked under it. I'll take it from there."

The old man grinned. The look he turned on me now was one of gleeful anticipation. He was satisfied that he was about to be proved right. The inspector would be bringing up incriminating prints and they would be mine. Much happier about the whole thing, he set about lifting the lining. Since he had already determined that the lining paper had been stretched irreparably, there seemed to be no reason for attacking it with loving care—no reason but the lifelong work habits of a superb craftsman. Working with magnificent precision, he detached the lining from the case.

Taking over from the old man, the inspector reached in under the detached lining with a small pair of tweezers and withdrew a sealed envelope. On the envelope was typed my name, nothing more.

Dusting the envelope front and back, he examined it for prints. There were none. Shaking the dust from the envelope, he opened it with his bare hands, but for removing its contents, he again resorted to the tweezers. He brought out a sheet of paper with something of a greater bulk folded inside it. Unfolding the paper, he revealed a second envelope and on the inner surface of the folded paper several lines of typing.

Before reading anything, he dusted both sides of the paper and both sides of that inner envelope. No prints or even blurred fragments of prints came up on any of the surfaces. Again he set the tweezers aside. The inner envelope was also sealed. This one had the inspector's name typed on it. The covering note read:

"Dear Bagby: Please do not open the enclosed envelope. If at the time you come on this I am still alive and able to communicate, then please bring it to me unopened and I will explain. If, however, I will have disappeared or should be dead or so severely injured that there will be no way of getting through to me, then surely you will appreciate the necessity of delivering the enclosed to your friend, Inspector Schmidt. He will want it. Nobody knows that you have it, but be most careful and get it into the inspector's hands without losing a moment. These people have ways of learning things that neither you nor I could ever imagine, and to get their hands on this they will stop at nothing. I know this is an imposition and I'm sorry about that, but you must believe me. I had nobody else I could turn to, nobody else I could trust. Somehow I never had the opportunity to tell you how greatly I have always admired you. It is late for that now, but better late than never."

It closed with "your friend, always your friend" and was signed with an indecipherable scrawl.

The three of us—the inspector, the old man, and I—read it together. The old man was the first to speak. Schmitty was studying the signature, and I was waiting for what he would say.

"You got a friend like that," the old man said, "I don't want to know what your enemies do to you."

"Maybe he thought we were friends," I said. "I never did. He was just a lug I knew."

"What about the signature?" Schmitty asked. "It could be anything. I'll need samples."

"It looks all right," I said.

"It looks like so much nothing at all."

"I know. About a week ago I was signing a petition. A guy in the club trying to get on the ballot for state senator. His friends are passing the petition around to everyone in the man's district. It happened they hit me right after they'd gotten Monroe's signature. Signing right on the next line I couldn't help noticing the crazy scrawl. I asked who and they said Lansing Monroe. If it looked like anything, it looked like what we have here."

"Okay," the inspector said, setting the note aside and ripping open his envelope. "Let's see what we do have."

Again there was the short delay before he read the contained note. He used the tweezers for removing it from the envelope and he dusted both sides of the paper, again with negative results, not even the smudged fragmentary remains of what might have once been a print. Only after this thorough examination did he set himself to read it.

Less generous than I had been, he wasn't sharing it with the old man and me. Drawing aside with it, he asked me to pack up his kit for him and suggested that I might use the few moments for arranging the repair of the slipcase.

While I repacked the kit, the old man was bringing out samples of paper, looking for one he would consider an adequate substitute for the ruined lining. I packed the kit up and joined him.

"Anything happened to the guy?" he asked.

"Lansing Monroe. Don't you read the papers or even watch the TV news?"

"There are better things to do."

"He was murdered. Machine gun—it just about cut him in half."

The old man winced. "A couple of minutes ago," he said, "I would have been saying it was no more than he deserved, but it would have been just a way of speaking. Nobody should be killed."

"Yes," I said. "That's what Inspector Schmidt is all about."

"He going to catch who did it?"

"He'll do his best, and most times his best is good enough."

We turned to discussing the papers. I left the choice to him and he chose a beauty. I expected the insurance company would be unhappy about the price, but he startled me by quoting a most modest figure.

"That is," he said, "if I can keep the old lining."

He could salvage enough of it to line a case for a smaller volume and that would cover the cost of the replacement paper. He was charging me only for his labor. We shook on that.

The inspector was outside waiting in the car. I joined him. As he pulled away from the curb, he handed me the note.

"It was better for the old guy not to read this," he said. "The job he's doing for you is an unusual event in his life. He's going to be talking about it and he'll be safer not knowing what it says there. I doubt that he ever gets his head out of his job long enough to have any idea of how dangerous it can be to be talking about Fats Jenkins."

"Monroe is fingering Jenkins?"

"Read it. You know when to talk and when to shut up."

I read:

"Dear Inspector Schmidt: You never knew me. By the time you have this, unless I had disappeared, you will probably have seen what they've left of me, regardless of whether it's my dead body or something more or something less. The way they operate, it's not impossible that they will have carted me off some place outside your jurisdiction and done it to me there. In that case, you'll know where this information should go. Although we didn't know each other, we did share a good friend, George Bagby. I left this with George because I knew of no surer way of getting it into your hands if or when it would become necessary that you have it.

"If it shall be that I have been killed, or that an all-but-successful attempt has been made on my life, it will be done by someone I cannot now identify for you. I have no expectation that Fats Jenkins will, with his own hands, pull the trigger or plunge the knife, but it will have been done on his orders. Whether by a killer hired for the one job or by one of the retinue of bully boys he always keeps around him I'm afraid you'll need to determine. I can tell you only what I know. Jenkins wants me dead and I have reason to believe that the life expectancy of anyone Jenkins wants dead is, to say the least, lousy.

"Jenkins has been supplying me with cocaine for which I have been paying and paying well. I have never quibbled about price. I have never delayed payment. I have never tried to avoid payment. He can have no complaint against me on that score. For some reason unknown to me he has come down with the conviction that someone is informing on him, and he has made up his mind that it is me. I have been totally unsuccessful in persuading him otherwise.

"Inspector, I am not an informer. You can see that from this letter. I am not going to you or to the Federal narcotics-men to ask for protection in exchange for my informing on Jenkins. That might be the sensible thing to do, but it goes against the grain. I can't make myself do it. I am taking this way of protecting myself. I hope it works. In that event, you will never see this letter. I am going to tell Jenkins I have written it and that it is safe with someone I can trust. I will tell him that nobody will ever read it so long as I come to no harm. I will make him understand that his safety depends on my safety.

"I know Jenkins. He operates on the assumption that he can do anything with impunity because he can always buy himself out of the consequences. I am doing this in a way that guarantees that it will come to you with no chance of its getting lost on the way, and I will let Jenkins know that because even in his assumptions there is the one exception. Inspector Schmidt cannot be bought."

It was signed with the same indecipherable scrawl, but under the signature here the name was typed—Lansing Monroe.

I read all of it before I spoke. "Mallory said he was into drugs," I said.

"Fats Jenkins?"

"No. Monroe."

"Dealing?"

"Why dealing?" I asked. "All he says here is he was buying from Jenkins. He says nothing about selling."

Schmitty laughed. "He does say he wasn't an informer. It went against the grain. Even informing on himself as a voice from the grave he didn't sing much of a tune. Even then, I guess, it went against the grain."

"But why should you be thinking he was dealing? Since he was so filthy rich, what would he have wanted with that?"

"It's a well-known way of getting filthy rich."

"When I suggested just that," I said, "you knocked it down. You said a man who had a steady supply of sure-fire money-making market tips didn't have to fool around with drug dealing. He had a better way."

"But now I have this statement that he bought from Fats Jenkins, every indication that they had a one-on-one arrangement."

"If he was buying, he had to buy from someone."

"Nobody," the inspector said, "can be such a heavy user that, if he's buying just for himself, he'll ever be making the big-quantity buys that would bring him within miles of Jenkins. If Jenkins is in that business, a guy would have to be a major dealer to come anywhere near him. Any ordinary buy, even the biggest of personal buys, would be done from someone way down the line, umpteen layers away from the big man himself."

"Then where did the market tips come from?"

"Nothing pinned down tight yet in any direction," the inspector said, "but now we have another possibility to look at."

"Okay," I said. "How about letting me have a look?"

"Cocaine," he said. "Expensive, and the drug of choice for the upper classes."

"So?"

"So let's say Monroe had broker friends, the big boys, the insiders. For them playing the market doesn't mean what it means to other people. They don't play it like it was a roulette wheel. They play it like it was a fiddle or a harp. They have a comfortable arrangement with Monroe. He supplies them with cocaine. They supply him with the word on when they're going to push a stock up and when they're going to let it drop and speed it on its way down. It saves them from having to do business with anyone lower class."

"You pulling Fats in?"

"On no more than this? I couldn't hold him long enough to make it worthwhile."

"Then what are you going to do?"

"Ask Narcotics if they've had any indication of Jenkins being into cocaine. If they haven't, and I'm pretty sure they haven't, I'll start them looking. As evidence, what we have here is just about worthless."

"It's a lead," I said.

"Is it? I take this to the DA and tell him how it was planted on you. You know what he's going to say?"

"He'll say bring Fats Jenkins in."

"No, he won't. He didn't go to law school for nothing. He'll tell me that what I've got here is so crazy that it isn't worth a dime.

The way this letter was planted was the act of a lunatic. So how do you convince a jury that the letter is anything but the ravings of a lunatic? If you want to have evidence believed, you have to be able to make it look like believable evidence."

CHAPTER 9

I had been waiting long for that drink and dinner. The waiting had, in fact, expanded my need from drink to drinks. Inspector Schmidt, however, was backing away from anything so civilized. He was having a change of mind. Even while he was telling me we could take little stock in the letter, he was not prepared to disregard it.

"I'll be wanting you with me tomorrow when I'll be talking with old McLeod and Junior; but first I have to do my homework. I'll need anything the boys have been digging up on Monroe. I also want to take another look at what they gave me on Bosco Griffiths and his bride before we talk to those two. I'll grab a couple of hamburgers at my desk."

I complained that I hadn't had a decent meal all day, but Schmitty knocked that off with his assurance that it would be no loss if I didn't go downtown with him. He would just be getting Narcotics moving on the possibility that the Jenkins mob had moved in on the cocaine traffic. The rest would be no more than paper work. If there should be anything in that, he could tell me about it in the morning.

"Call it a day, kid. Tell me where you want to eat. I'll drop you."

"Make it the club."

He checked on whether I had my key to his apartment on me.

I had it. I told him I hoped I wouldn't be using it.

"Mattress delivery was promised for this afternoon," I said. "I'll go home after dinner and attack the mess. I still have to make chaos out of chaos, and I've hardly started. That way, when I poop out, I can just fall into bed."

The inspector leaves nothing to chance. He told me exactly what I was to do in the event that the mattresses hadn't been delivered.

"Tell the cop that's in there now that you won't be sleeping there tonight. He'll alert precinct to expect a call from you when you're ready to pull out for my place. They'll have a man right over to take the night watch. Don't leave until he gets there."

"How long are we going to go on with this, Schmitty?"

"Just tonight. I'll have a man over first thing in the morning to change your locks."

I had a solitary dinner and took my drinks at the table. I had run it too close to the time when they would be closing the club dining room to do it any other way. There was no time for anything like the usual convivial prelude in the bar. I wasn't regretting it. Although I wanted to relax over the meal, I didn't want to let the time run on as it will when you are in company. I wanted to get home and start coping with the monumental disorder.

At the apartment the mattresses hadn't been delivered. The cop who'd been standing guard told me that there had been a call for me shortly after he had come on.

"It was the store," he said. "They said to tell you they couldn't make it today. They promised for sure tomorrow."

"Great," I said. "They also promised for sure today."

I followed Schmitty's instructions and told him I wouldn't be staying the night and I would be calling precinct before I would leave.

Having seen him to the door, I returned to the bedroom. I had been thinking of stripping down to the waist and having at it, but the prospect of having to dress again to go over to Schmitty's seemed too much. I had lost all interest in staying long or doing much. I left it with loosening my tie and letting it dangle and opening the top button of my shirt.

I picked the empty drawers off the floor and fitted them back into the chests. Then I made a start on picking up the shirts and such that had been dumped out of them. Before I'd more than begun on returning them to the drawers, I had to take time out to answer the doorbell.

I went to the door with the hope that the Sleep Shop had found its way to making a late-evening delivery. It was only by way of preparing myself for disappointment that I played with the thought that it would probably only be Josiah McLeod, Jr., come again to tell me about the viscosity of blood. In retrospect I can think that I should have approached that door warily, but I had been alerted only to the possibility of someone who might come with a key. A burglar doesn't ring the bell unless it is in an effort to ascertain that the premises are empty. If there is no answer, he goes in. If there is an answer, he apologizes, mumbling something about having the wrong address, and takes off. Since I had never been fully convinced even of the threat from a man with a key, it was with blithe unconcern that I opened the door.

Saying that I opened it is something of an overstatement. I did no more than unlock it. All of the rest was out of my hands. The door came swinging in. It came with such great speed and force that it hit me full in the face. It was a stunning blow that sent me staggering backward. The impact of the door would have knocked me flat if it hadn't been that my visitor came with it. Flinging an arm around me, he held me upright and hugged me tight against him.

I had a moment or two of blurred vision and addled wits. I can remember feeling nothing and thinking nothing except for a vague gratitude to this man who was saving me from collapsing to the floor. With some dim notion of feeling my face to assess damage—I had visions of flattened nose, blackened eyes, and cut lips—I tried to raise my hand.

Only then did it occur to me to question the benevolence of the bear hug. Pressed tight against the man's extraordinarily hard body, my one arm was pinned to my side. The other hand, however, was also immobilized. It had been grabbed at the wrist and was being held bent across my back.

Recognizing that much had an instantaneously settling effect on me. My head cleared. It is probable that my vision cleared at the same time. About that I cannot say. We were pressed so close together that our faces were all but touching. At such proximity you just can't focus. Though seeing wasn't any good, there was nothing wrong with feeling. The hardness of the man's body pressed against me was too strange. It was unlike anything in nature unless you wanted to think in terms of turtles, crabs, and lobsters. The hardest-muscled superathlete is never so steely hard, and however hard-bodied he might be, it is quite impossible that the muscle sheath of his chest and abdomen should be harder than his biceps. It wasn't body that I was feeling tight against me. It was armor. The man was wearing a bulletproof vest.

It was not only like steel, it was steel. Simultaneously with this recognition I had another, and it was also of steel and also pressed against me. Although I had never before had it in precisely that same disconcerting place, I'd had it and nobody needed to tell me what it was. It was a gun muzzle. This performance of holding me helpless with the power of just his left hand and arm wasn't empty showing off. He had employment for his right hand.

You probably have heard about the way a gun can be handled if anyone makes the mistake of training one on you at close quarters. It's the quick pivot and the arm slicing down to strike his wrist. An arm moves faster than a trigger finger. You may even have taken a self-defense course where they taught you how to do it.

That is all very well if your man is close enough for your flailing arm to strike his wrist but not so close that he's left you no room in which your arm can flail. My man wasn't giving me sufficient room. He was giving me no room at all. Furthermore, he was leaving me no arm to flail with.

You are now probably trying to visualize some vital spot on my body where in that situation I could be feeling the pressure of his gun muzzle. My head? If he ever thought of that, I expect he would have rejected it as too merciful.

He had come at me in a slight crouch. He was a big guy, considerably taller than me. Despite the fact that he was in a crouch and I was upright, the top of his head was about at a level with my eyes. There was something strange about his head, but I couldn't give any thought to trying to understand that. Just then I had other preoccupations.

I suppose that crouched down the way he was, it would have been clumsy to reach up and hold a gun to my head. I couldn't, however, even for a moment believe that he had settled for any mere target of convenience. Everything was telling me that it was the target of deliberate, sadistic choice. He was down where, even in that close embrace, he had room for his right hand and the gun. He was between my thighs with the gun muzzle pressing upward.

"Listen, Mr. Detective," he said, "and listen good."

There was nothing wrong with my listening, but I had heard enough.

"You're making a mistake," I said.

"No, Mr. Detective, it's you is making the mistake. It's a bad mistake you don't listen when I got a gun on you. My buddy, he's in back of you, he's got a gun on you, too." I started to turn my head. Anyone behind me must have come there by pushing past us in the doorway. I'd had no awareness of it, but I couldn't be certain it hadn't happened during those first moments when I'd been too befuddled to register properly on anything. Now, twisting my captive wrist as he stepped up the pressure of his gun muzzle, he commanded my full attention. "You can play along with us or we can blow you away," he said. "It's all the same to us."

"I'm not a detective," I said. "It's all a mistake, a crazy, old man's mistake."

"Hey, Buddy," he said. "Mr. Detective here needs reasoning with. Come in close and leave him know you're there. Give him the feel of your gun. Shove it up his ass. That'll do it."

Buddy was back there. Although he didn't follow the instructions to the letter, he did let me feel his gun muzzle, jabbing me with it at the base of my spine. A shot taken there mightn't leave you dead, but it will leave you with a paralysis that will make you wish you were.

Somewhere in there I came to know what was strange about the lug's face. I hadn't been giving it any thought. I didn't have any thinking that could be spared for something so trifling, not at that time. It just came to me. He had a nylon stocking pulled down over his head. Stockings put to such use were no novelty. They make an effective mask. They have the added advantage of being easily carried and, after they are no longer needed, easily disposed of.

There was nothing for me to do but play for time. I hadn't the first idea of what I could do with time. I knew only that I wanted it.

"Who are you?" I asked. "What do you want?"

"Never no mind who we are. For now all we want is you listen and you do just like teacher says. Teacher don't want to get tough and you don't want him to get tough. You ready to be a good boy?"

"I'm listening."

"We're going places and we're taking you with us. If you don't want to come, you don't have to. We'll just leave you here for the meat wagon to come and cart you away to the morgue. All you got to do is come along quietly like we was pals going out for a night on the town. You don't say nothing. You don't do nothing. Later on it'll get to be your time to talk and then we'll listen. You behave yourself until then and you talk good then and you won't get hurt none. You don't talk good and you'll get hurt like you never been hurt. Don't get to thinking we don't know how. We're specialists. You don't want samples even."

"It's no good my telling you you're making a mistake?"

"You already told me. I'm telling you. I don't make mistakes. Like they say, they put erasers on pencils. They don't put no erasers on bullets. Bullets are for keeps."

I could see only one glimmer of hope. If there would be that time when it would be my turn to speak and theirs to listen, I might find words to convince them. It was certainly the faintest of glimmers, but I was telling myself that it was all I had.

"You're calling it," I said.

"We have a car outside. We're going out and we're getting into the car. My friend will be right with you all the way. You make even the smallest wrong move and he'll leave you have it. You'll be shut of us if that's the way you want it, but you'll also be laying dead in the gutter. I'll have the car door open. You'll go straight for it and right in. You will not turn your head. You will look straight ahead all the time. That goes for all the time starting right now."

"I can do that," I said.

"I know you can. Will you?"

"I will."

The gun pressed into my back came away; but it was only for a moment or two before it was back with renewed pressure. It took a painful muscular effort to hold my head rigid and keep it from turning to see what the man had been doing with that tiny interval of time. I'd had my orders. I was being a model of obedience.

Almost immediately, however, I knew the answer. As soon as the gun rammed back into my spine, the man who had taken me face to stocking-masked face let go of my wrist and released me from his imprisoning hug. Simultaneously he jumped backward, taking his gun off me and putting it at a distance that was just beyond my reach.

Ramming it into his shoulder holster, he turned toward the door. He just turned. Before he made any further move forward, he paused and, standing with his back to me, he pulled the stocking off his head and stuffed it in his pocket. I could now guess that his companion had just been doing the same. Removal of the stockings took two hands.

They were not taking any chance in going out to the street masked, not even for the few steps it would take them to make it from my doorstep to their car. It was essential for them, however, that I not see their faces. It would be for that reason that turning my head would be an offense punishable by death.

If I was to keep my head rigidly faced forward, he was holding his to no less strict a constraint. He could have been a soldier on parade as he went to the door, opened it, and, leaving it ajar, went out to the street. His companion shifted the pressure of his gun muzzle away from my spine, applying it to my side at a point just below the rib cage. His free arm he flung across my shoulders in what would look like affectionate companionability. If I'd had no other indication by which I could have known better, the feel of it could have told me. He was positioned so that his face was beside my ear—neatly beyond any area that even the most extensively peripheral vision could encompass.

The impulse to turn my head that very little bit it would have taken was all but irresistible, but I had been warned. The warning sufficed to stiffen my resistance. We marched together out to the street.

"Close your door," he said, holding me briefly on the doorstep.

His lips were so close that I felt his breath warm and moist on my ear. I had to turn to pull the door shut and I was wondering whether I could get away with making the turn in his direction and catching a glimpse of his face. I would, after all, be turning on his orders.

Before I had made even the beginning of a move, however, I had reasoned myself away from any such folly. I might have done it, and it might have seemed that I had gotten away with it. I would have been permitted the delusion until they would have been satisfied that I had told them everything I knew, but only until then. Anyone who could recognize these bastards would never be left alive to testify against them. I was telling myself that it was even more to my interest than to theirs that I not see their faces.

In any event that arm across my shoulders left me no question about which way I was to turn. Actually I was being given no option. I was being turned. These buckos were professionals. They had the unfailing eye for detail. They missed out on nothing.

I closed the door but I managed a little something. For whatever it might be worth as a signal I contrived it so that it was only closed. It wasn't locked. The other guy was waiting at the car, holding the door open but bent down as though examining a scratch in the paintwork.

Just as I began climbing in, my escort took over. The back seat was empty, but it was not for me to occupy it. A mighty push sent me sprawling face down on the car floor. A hand grabbed a large fistful of the hair at the back of my head and made it serve as a handle for controlling the movements of my head.

Did I say these guys were pros? Their expertise was awesome. My head was lifted to bring my face away from the car floor but it was so pointed that I had nothing to see but a folded-back jump-seat. Dangling there were long, broad strips of adhesive tape. To each of two of the tapes was fastened a pillowy mass.

It was obvious that all of that would have been prepared for me. Even as I was wondering how it was to be used, I was entertaining the vain hope that by some miracle I might never know. I had only a moment for the wondering. The hope was immediately destroyed. I got to see what they were doing with one of the two elaborated tapes. While one of those bimbos controlled me by kneeling on me and using both his hands to hold my head still, the other adjusted the thick wad of gauze over my eyes and secured it by winding the tape around my head.

I was blindfolded. With no further need to control my head movements, they switched me to a position which permitted them to work more comfortably. The rest of it went rapidly.

The second padded mass, of course, was a gag. It was forced into my mouth and its lengths of tape were wound around my head to hold it secure. The remaining tapes bound me at wrists, ankles, elbows, and knees. My arms had been bound behind my back and the tapes at my wrists were firmly secured to those at my ankles. They had me compactly packaged for lying on my side on the car floor between front seat and back.

Transported thus through the streets of Manhattan, I was wishing they hadn't paid me the compliment of thinking that I might have had the courage or, if you like, the foolhardiness to make any move against them when I would be making it in the face of their all-too-explicit threat of murder. In retrospect, however, I am forced to recognize, if not to admire, their mastery of the techniques of kidnapping.

They had me immobilized and out of sight. Unmasked they could drive with impunity through the city streets, showing nothing that could arouse suspicion. They had no need to fear anything from a passing police car or from even the most sharply observant good citizen.

The drive seemed to go on forever, but under the circumstances my estimates of time were worthless. In any situation of extreme anxiety minutes become eternities; but, even allowing for such distortions of judgment, I couldn't escape the recognition that we were driving a long way. I was trying to keep track of the route we were taking—turns and distances and all that—but for the most part I achieved nothing more than confusion.

We made left turns and right turns but in the city, where you can make turns at every corner and they all feel alike, they told me nothing. I could count our stops for traffic lights, but what would there have been to make of the sum? There are traffic lights at every corner. For some time I couldn't even tell whether we were going any great distance or if they were merely confusing me by going up one street and down another, making next to nothing seem like very much.

Then there was a change. The character of the sounds changed and we were going a long way without any stops for traffic lights. That told me something. We had left the city streets for a highway, but which of the many, headed in what direction?

When eventually a couple of clues came my way, they came to my nose. The first was an unmistakable stench. If you are or have been a farm boy, you'd probably know it. I am not and I never have been, but living in New York and having frequent occasion to drive out of the city and across New Jersey, I know that when I am coming into the vicinity of the town of Secaucus, I must roll up the car windows. Secaucus has pig farms. I don't know how near these farms are to the New Jersey Turnpike, but I have never driven out that way when the winds have not been drenching the road with the Secaucus aroma.

I didn't want to believe it. I was trying not to think about that line in the strange letter—if Monroe's slaughtered corpse had turned up some place out of his jurisdiction, Schmitty would have known to whom he was to give his information. Across the river and into New Jersey—this was not only away from the inspector's Manhattan field of operations, it was even out of the state. I told myself that I had no absolute proof. Along some highway with which I was less familiar there might be a point at which the road passed a similar concentration of pig farms.

I told myself to forget it. It made no difference. All I had established was that we were not going up and down city streets to create for me by making much out of nothing an illusion of going far afield. We were out of town and headed for some remote area, undoubtedly for some isolated spot. Whether in one direction or another made no difference. What would be making the difference would be whether the isolated spot had been chosen as a good place for holding me for questioning or as a desirable place for a murder.

We drove out of the area of pig stench and, after what seemed like another succession of eternities, my nose presented me with the second piece of information. This time it was a different stench, the polluting fumes put out by oil-cracking plants. I can't say that this recognition made me feel good. In my situation nothing could have made me feel good. That petroleum reek, nevertheless, did make me feel better. It couldn't alleviate the seeming hopelessness of my predicament, but coming out of total disorientation brought for me, however irrationally, some small relief.

I now had two fixed points—Secaucus and Linden. If you haven't forgotten your geometry, you know that two points determine a line. I had my line. It was without question the New Jersey Turnpike. There might have been two highways out of New York that went by pig farms, but two highways where the pig farms were followed at an interval by oil-cracking plants were completely unlikely.

That after Linden we continued on the Turnpike for what seemed to be a considerable distance was in no way out of line with what I had been thinking. We were going out beyond the Jersey meadows and the industrial suburbs, beyond the dormitory communities of suburbia, heading at least for the more open areas of exurbia if not for the farm and wood-lot country beyond.

Ordinarily, one thinks of that country out there as an area of peace and quiet, of delightfully pastoral privacy. On that ride I was seeing it differently. It was a territory for torture where no one would hear the victim's screams of agony. It was the perfect natural setting for murder.

When we made a brief stop, I heard the clink of coins. We were leaving the Turnpike. The stop had been for the tollbooth. I had a faint and only momentary flicker of hope. The man in the elevated perch of the tollbooth was in a position to look down into the car. From that angle of vision he just might see me trussed up on the car floor.

Alone and unarmed, he would hardly be taking any action on his own. I knew that. He might, however, make a quick call to the police and set off a search if not even a pursuit. My kidnappers had left me down there uncovered. I was asking myself if that could have been their mistake.

I was working my imagination hard in an effort to construct in my mind a picture of the relative positions. It was discouraging. For paying the toll the car pulls up with the driver directly alongside the toll taker. That's essential for passing up the money and handing down the change. Looking down into the car, the toll taker can see into the driver's area. The floor in back is out of his range. It will come into his line of vision only in passing, when the toll has been paid and the car is pulling away. Then it will be only for a moment and in that moment he would still have to be looking down and not already switching his attention to the next car in line.

Even my small hope died a quick death. The car shot away from the booth in a racing start. There would have been time to see nothing.

CHAPTER 10

It had seemed reasonable enough that, once we were off the Turnpike and on to relatively unpoliced country roads, the driving should become less circumspectly lawful. I hadn't, however, anticipated so abrupt and immediate a shift from the sober to a reckless pace; but, when it did happen, it didn't occur to me that it could be in any way significant. A man of reckless temperament, disciplined to be professionally cautious, could at the first opportunity be expected to break out into his natural ways.

Professional wisdom dictated that with the passenger he was carrying he could permit himself to do nothing that might get him pulled over for even a mild warning. I could easily imagine that in the city streets and on the Turnpike he had been chafing under the restraints he had been forced to accept. Having at long last reached the place where he could break free from such restraints, might he not quite naturally explode out of them?

We hit a winding road and were careening along it at what had to be suicidal speed. I could sense that from the degree of centrifugal force exerted on me on each turn. My trussed-up body was banging hard against first one car door and then the other. Only if you are flying around turns do you generate that much swing. Also, the turns followed one on the other at too frequent intervals. Roads just aren't built that way. Even on the spectacular twisters like the Grand Corniche and the Amalfi Drive there is some interval between turns. I know the state of New Jersey well. For a Manhattanite it's virtually his back yard. It has no such hazardous spectaculars. This hazard could be arising only from monstrously excessive speed.

I began to think that, whether it had been in the orders or not, I was not going to come out of this ride alive. I couldn't, however, believe that the orders could have been that in the process of rubbing me out, my kidnappers were to go over the edge with me.

It was only when the shooting started that I began to think I understood. A revolver shot fired a hundred feet away can be mistaken for an automobile exhaust. A shot pulled off less than two feet from your ear makes an unmistakable sound. The man who was not doing the driving had to be kneeling on the front seat and shooting back over my head.

Possibly less easily identifiable was the sound of the return fire. There was a sound and it brought out of memory an experience of many years before, an exercise I had been put through as a part of army training. To give us the experience of moving under hostile fire we were set to crawling across a field under controlled fire, aimed to pass over the heads of the crawling troops. I can remember crossing that field with my buttons digging a trench under me while I prayed that the fire was indeed controlled. It was an unforgettable experience, and now I was being most forcibly reminded of the sound of those passing slugs.

This would be it, if only I could survive. There would be no question but that I would stay down. I had learned that and learned it well in the army exercise. There was, however, an important difference. Across that field I had been self-propelled. Now along this winding road I had no control. I was being moved.

I tried to keep my mind off that. I was telling myself that I had underestimated the man in the Turnpike tollbooth. He had looked down into the car and he had a remarkably quick eye and a quick understanding. He had rung through to the police. They had tracked us, and they were giving chase. They were not going to lose us. They would be taking us in dead or alive. I much preferred that it should be alive.

Since I could play it only by ear, I had to do some guessing at what was going on. When there was a change in the firing, I was immediately aware of the change. It became one-sided, all of it coming from our pursuers. I could only guess that the guy who had been returning their fire had paused to reload. I had kept no count of his shots. Even if I'd thought to attempt it, I doubt that it could have been possible.

If anything, the driving now stepped up to even wilder insanity. It seemed to me that the reloading was taking a very long time. Even allowing for the way the distortions of anxiety will stretch the minutes, I began to think that even a man who'd never had a weapon in his hands before couldn't be so long about getting it loaded. It was impossible for that to apply to either of my kidnappers. I had to conclude that the wild careening of our ride was tossing him about so much that he was being slowed up.

Then everything stopped. It stopped with an ear-shattering, bone-rattling bang. I may have been knocked unconscious, but I think not. I think I just had a moment of being dazed and befuddled. I came out of it into what seemed to be complete stillness. I had the quick first thought that this could be the stillness of death, but I took a long breath and knew I was alive.

A large assortment of small aches asserted themselves. My ears did a recovery from that shattering shock. They began picking up on small sounds. Any sounds would have seemed small after that big blast. There was the rustling of leaves in the wind. Somewhere an owl hooted. I was listening for human sounds. Even if my kidnappers were saying nothing, it was inconceivable that the police shouldn't be coming up to take them. The firing had stopped and the car had stopped.

I could not take that for anything but surrender. I was coming to realize that the car had stopped in the way that had been inevitable. That it could have gone on forever without missing on one of the turns and crashing into something had been impossible. That it had gone on for as long as it had was at least extraordinary. Now, however, it had happened. I was developing a mental picture. The car was wrecked. The chase was over.

Even though I had been listening in expectation of human sounds, when the shout came without even so much as a preliminary rustle and only inches away from my ear, it made me jump. It was, of course, a severely restricted jump, more like a convulsive twitch within my bounds.

It was some moments before I had any intelligent grasp of the words. The first of them, therefore, are something like a reconstruction.

"Come on in. You can quit covering me. They ain't ever again going to give nobody no trouble. We got the one of them. The other one took care of hisself. He went through the windshield. What he was using for a brain, it's splattered all over. It couldn't have been much. Bulletproof vest and no seat belt, the dope."

"Dead?"

"The both of them. Sure."

"What about him? He all right?"

I was convinced that my assortment of aches came from nothing that was not minor. I wanted to tell them that I was all right, but I would have needed to be rid of the gag first. I felt that I had taken a considerable banging, but I was sure I hadn't broken anything.

I felt hands on me, cautious hands, gentle in their touch. They were feeling for heart beat and for breathing.

"Can you hear me, Mr. Bagby?"

I nodded.

"Are you all right?"

I nodded.

"Are you hurt anywhere?"

I shook my head. The little aches, even though they were numerous, didn't call for a nod.

Then there was another voice. This one had also come up close.

"Geeezzuss! You ain't going to get him out of all them without you're going to tear all the skin off of him."

"You just watch me. All I need is you got that Boy Scout knife of yours on you, the one's got the scissors on to it."

"It ain't no Boy Scout knife. It's a Swiss Army knife."

"Swiss Army, Swiss Navy. I don't give a damn. Just leave me have it."

He began by cutting the tapes that fastened my ankles to my wrists. I was grateful for anything, but I would have preferred other priorities. The lad who had provided the Swiss Army knife spoke for me. He might have been reading my mind.

"He could wait for that," he said. "First thing he'll want, it's his mouth and his eyes."

"That's how much you know. First thing he's wanting is to piss unless he's wet hisself already."

If the one had been reading my mind, this one was reading the rest of me and, of course, he was right. He was now working on the tapes that bound my ankles. He was making no effort to pull them off. He just cut them. It served well enough for freeing my legs.

The other guy needed to be right about something. "He'll be too stiff and cramped to stand on his own," he said. "We'll have to help him."

"I know. We'll get him on his feet and you hold him up while I cut his arms free."

Together they lifted me out of the car and stood me on my feet. They were right. Without their support I would have gone down. My legs were not only stiff and cramped, but there was no communication between them and the rest of me. Cutting the next set of tapes freed my knees and communication began. Just then it was not yet useful communication. It was only the pain of the returning blood flow.

The man with the little scissors was working rapidly and efficiently. He cut the tape at my wrists and freed my arms. All of this was taking no more than seconds, but I didn't have many more seconds to spare. My hands were once more mine but, hurrying to unzip, I learned immediately that it was going to be some time before my numbed fingers could be of any use to me. They were getting nowhere. They just fumbled futilely.

A hand came in and pushed mine aside. With the concerned gentleness of a father assisting a newly housebroken little boy, there was done for me what I was then incapable of doing for myself.

"Okay, Mr. Bagby," my kind and gentle benefactor said, "leave it go."

Leaving me to it, he turned his attention to cutting the tapes that were holding the gag fixed to my mouth. That was the more deli-

cate job. Since up there the tapes had not been cutting off circulation, I could feel the smooth edge of the scissors against the skin of
my face. He was working the scissors with the greatest care.

When he had freed the thing at one side, he pulled the wad out
of my mouth and just left it to dangle alongside my chin. I had to
spit before I could speak.

"Thanks," I said. "You guys are great. You've been marvelous.
You can be sure I'll tell the inspector."

"Just doing our job," one of them said.

"Glad to do it," said the other.

"There are lots of ways a job like yours can be done," I said.
"Most of them don't pack thoughtful kindness and consideration in
along with the efficiency."

I was ready to zip up. Feeling was back in my hands, but as it
had been in my feet and legs, here at the start it was mostly pain. I
did, however, have some control of my fingers. Although their response was sluggish and given to a degree of fumbling, with concentration I was managing. One of them asked if I could handle it
or if I needed help.

"I'll do it," I said. "I'm making progress. It'll be almost no time at
all before I'm toilet trained."

As jokes go, this was no gut-buster, but from a stand-up comic
who could hardly stand without assistance, I suppose it was good
enough. They roared with laughter. They slapped me on the back.
They told me I was a lot of man. It was their joint opinion that
most men put through even half of what I'd had that night would
have been shaking wrecks in need of sedation. They wouldn't have
been making jokes.

The boy who had been working the scissors was the first to bring
himself down to sobriety. Talking past a few residual chuckles
which he firmly suppressed, he told me I would have to hold absolutely still for a while and not even speak.

"Even just talking," he said, "it'll move your face a little. I'm
going to try to get the damn blindfold off of you and it's going to
be tricky. You ain't going to thank me none if I stick the scissors in
your eye."

"Right," I said. "I'd rather you didn't."

He worked at it for what I judged to be several minutes, trying to find a place around my eyes where he could slip the scissors blade between the tape and my skin. He was working nerve-wrackingly close to my eyes and, as far as I could judge from what I felt and from the steady stream of his muttered obscenities, I knew that he was getting nowhere with it. I was more than ready to have him give up on that endeavor long before he would declare himself defeated.

"Sorry, Mr. Bagby," he said. "The way this is giving me the shakes, I can't trust myself with the scissors no more. It's going to have to wait till we get where we can have a better scissors, the kind that ain't got a point on it. This one here, it comes down to a point—it's sharp like a needle."

"Forget about cutting it," I said. "Just yank the tape off. I can take it."

"Yank it off?" The suggestion horrified him. "The way it's wrapped around your head, I can't pull it off without I scalp you. We're going to need some kind of solvent stuff to loosen it off of you before we go to pulling on it at all."

"Hair grows back in."

"Yeah. That's later, but first it's yanked out in bleeding clumps. You don't want it, and if I done anything like that to you, I'd get me skinned alive."

I'd been too long without seeing. I wanted the damn thing off.

"Not when I say that you did it only on my insistance," I said.

"Sorry, friend. Can't do. We've got our orders and we've got to follow them. We can't take no orders from you. It'll come off as soon as we get to where we can do it right."

They walked me to their car. It wasn't coercion. It felt like guidance. They couldn't have been more solicitous, guiding my footsteps, holding me by the arms and keeping me to the road. I did begin developing a small feeling that I might have been their prisoner, but I put it from me. I went beyond that. I accused myself of ingratitude. At worst, I told myself, I was the prisoner of their kindness and consideration.

They helped me into the car. One of them got into the back seat beside me. I heard the car door slammed shut and almost simultaneously I heard the slam of the second door and the sound of the engine starting up.

"What about them?" I asked, as I felt the car go through the maneuverings of a broken U-turn. "You just leaving them like that?"

The guy who was sharing the back seat with me gave me my answer.

"We should stop and keep you waiting while we dig them graves?" he said.

"They'll rot just as good where they are."

That came from the driver. He had completed the turn and we took off, back over that twisting road. We weren't taking it at anything like the suicidal speed of the drive in, but from the feel of it the car wasn't loafing. I kept flexing my fingers, working the numbness and the pain out of them, trying to hasten their return to full usefulness. I needed to have them fully functional if only on feel I was to locate the end of the tape and pick enough of it loose for a good finger-tip grip. They couldn't rip the tape off, but as soon as my hand would be ready I could be doing it for myself. I was going to free myself of the blindfold.

We came to some straighter going, made a very brief stop, negotiated a long, sweeping curve, and then settled into a straight, steady run. I didn't have to puzzle over that. The brief pause had been for plucking the Turnpike ticket out of the dispensing machine. The long, smooth curve had been the entrance ramp. We were back on the Turnpike. I assumed we were headed back toward the city.

"Aren't you calling in a report?" I asked.

"Reporting can wait. First thing is to get you where a doctor can look at you and we can get you fixed up."

"I don't need a doctor. I'm okay."

"We can't take any chances, Mr. Bagby. It's our necks."

So much solicitude was making me uncomfortable. It was excessive. I wasn't an emergency case. My life wasn't hanging by a thread.

My hands were feeling much better. I began feeling of the tape I had wrapped around my head. It was no good. The numbness was not yet sufficiently gone from my fingers. Feeling was still to come back into them sufficiently for me to locate the ends of the tape. I had to wait a little longer.

Time wore on and I took to sniffing the air, expecting my nose to tell me we were again passing Linden and the oil-cracking plants. My nose was telling me nothing and the feeling grew on me that we were not headed back to New York. We were going the other way. I tried to tell myself it figured. I'd been an idiot thinking they could have been some of Inspector Schmidt's boys. I suppose the only reason I'd ever had for thinking it was that it was what I wanted them to be. I put myself through the quick mental switch.

We were in New Jersey. They had caught up with my kidnappers in New Jersey. I should have realized immediately they would have to be Jersey cops if they weren't FBI. The inspector had put out the alarm and one of these other outfits had come through on it. That anyone had managed, that they had succeeded in picking up the trail, all seemed miraculous; but it was so welcome a miracle that I was in no way disposed to question it.

Try as I might, however, to put the questions from my mind, they kept coming at me and always more insistently. I know police officers—great ones, good ones, mediocre ones, slovenly ones, hopelessly incompetent ones. All I have known, even the hopelessly incompetent, have some degree of professionalism. These two who had come to my rescue merited an efficiency record that should have put them among the great ones, but there seemed to be something subtly unprofessional about them. There was nothing specific I could put my finger on, but it was there.

Now, however, as we rode on and on, I was becoming aware of specifics. Police cars are equipped for two-way communication. They could be reporting in without stopping even for a moment. Even before we had left the scene shouldn't they have called in to report that they had me and that I was okay? Also, shouldn't they have reported the two dead men and where the bodies could be picked up?

Such oddities should have hit me immediately. I can explain my being so long a time in thinking of them only by assuming that I'd been far more in shock than I had at the time realized. Now there was this long drive. We had left the Turnpike. I picked up on that just as I had the first time, except that this time it had been easier. The guy doing the driving had explained me to the toll taker. I suppose the man in the tollbooth had looked into the car and seen me. Sitting up on the seat, I'd been in plain view.

"We're taking our friend to where he can get all his bandages took off of him," my self-appointed friend said.

"Gee. The poor guy." The toll taker had been sympathetic.

I had sat there and said nothing. Now I was kicking myself for not having come to my senses earlier. We were again on a winding country road. I had to think that we were again headed for some isolated place. This wasn't Texas where it can be hundreds of miles between one habitation and the next. This was New Jersey. Even in its most rural parts, towns are never far apart. It's never any great jump between hospitals, police stations, State Police barracks. Where could cops be taking me that would involve this much driving?

"Where are we going?" I asked.

"We're almost there."

That was all the answer I was given. There was nothing impatient in the tone of it. It sounded as though they regarded me as a fretful child. They were soothing me.

I had to have the blindfold off. I don't know what I thought I could gain from seeing their faces, but it was a need I could no longer deny myself. I reached up and tried again. This time my hands were ready for it. I could feel the nicked-up end of the tape under my fingernails. I worked enough of it loose to afford me a good grip and began to pull.

That beginning would be the easy part. There it was only tape laid over tape. There would be a lot more unwinding to do before it would be pulling on hair. I had little more than started when my companion in the back seat grabbed my hands and pulled them away from my head.

"None of that, buddy," he said.

"Let go. It's my head."

"But it'll be our ass."

I broke out of his grip, but before I could even get a hand on the tape, he was again pulling my hand away. We were all over the back seat wrestling. I must have been too occupied with that to have noticed when the car pulled to the side of the road and stopped. The first I knew of it was when I had four hands on me. The driver had joined the battle and was taking command.

"Just hold him down a minute," he said, "till I get his belt off of him. We'll have to strap his hands down."

"He started to rip the tape off."

"Yeah, I know."

I could feel him working at my belt buckle. I was thrashing about. I was not going to make it easy for him.

"Calm down, brother," he said. "We don't like doing this to you, but you're making us do it. You won't be good, so there's nothing else we can do."

It was the gentlest kind of scolding. If they were being cruel, they wanted to have me know it was only to be kind. The one who was holding me down joined in. His was the same purring tone, benevolent but firm, the papa-knows-best and you'll-thank-me-for-this-one-day approach.

"It won't be so terrible," he said. "Your pants fit real nice. Even without the belt, they ain't going to fall down on you."

With the belt off me they joined forces in bringing me under control so they could bind my hands. Strapping my hands down to my sides was again done with their astonishing efficiency. They worked together in perfect team coordination. In a matter of moments my hands were again immobilized. There was a difference. This time the method was more humane.

Immediately the driver was back behind the wheel and he had the car rolling again. They weren't cops. I was convinced of that much, and I was trying to fit the whole mad performance into some comprehensible pattern. Who were these guys and why was I on their most-wanted list? The best I could make of it was an elaborate variant on the bad-guy-good-guy routine. I was thinking that the wild pursuit, the gun fight, and the crash had been nothing more than a prearranged phony. I had never seen the front end of the kidnap car. I was imagining something like a specially constructed bumper that could withstand a crash into a tree. It would give off a loud bang and send something like an earthquake tremor back through the car, more than enough to convince a trussed-up, sightless man who had been bounced about in the car. The shooting would have been carefully aimed to hit nobody, and nobody would have gone through the windshield.

The bad guys would have quietly stood by while the good guys took over with their extraordinary kindness and solicitude, a kindness and solicitude that even went so far as their refusal to subject me to the pain of removing the blindfold. That brutal method of securing the blindfold would have been part of the scheme since I was no more to see the faces of my rescuers than I had been to see those of my kidnappers.

There would have been no wrecked car and no bodies left to rot in it. My rescuers carried me off, and when we had gone, the bad guys, having finished playing their part, had driven away. I had seen no bodies and no wrecked car. On all of that I had only the word of these two clowns.

The more I worked at it, the more reasonable this picture came to seem. It even took the miracle out of something I had been accepting even though I had been haunted by the feeling that it might have been too miraculous. There had been the question of how the pursuers had managed to pick up on the kidnap car. If it had been a prearranged meeting, then nothing could have been easier.

The vital questions, however, remained unanswered. Who were these guys? Why should they have staged this insanely elaborate caper? What could they want of me that they could hope to have through this wildly complicated softening-up process?

"Who are you?" I asked.

"A couple of friends. We saved your life."

"Only that?"

"Ain't it enough? Ain't a guy's life a lot?"

"Why did you do it?"

"That's a stupid question. If you had you the chance you could save a man's life, what would you do? Turn your back and walk away?"

"What do you want of me?"

"Only that you behave yourself. We don't want we should have

to get rough with you. We like you. So all we want of you is you
don't give us no hard time and you don't make us hurt you none."

"That is until you have me delivered. Where are you taking me?"

"Where you can be checked over to make sure you're okay.
Where all that damn tape can be got off of you without hurting you
none."

"And when it's off, won't I be seeing faces I can later recognize
and identify?"

"You won't want to do that. It ain't like we'll be putting in for no
reward or like that."

"Virtue is its own reward," I said.

I'll never know whether they didn't recognize mockery or pre-
tended they didn't.

"Yeah. Like that. You know how to say things real nice."

In all fairness I must admit that I may have been the one who
wasn't recognizing mockery.

"But it's important that I don't see my good friends' faces."

"Buddy, you've gotten so you just can't trust nobody and I can't
blame you after what you been through with them guys, they took
you for a ride. You can't even trust the guys, they saved your life
for you."

"If that's what it was."

"If that's what what was?"

"Saving my life."

"If you can doubt it after the way they done you, brother, you'll
have to take our word for it. If it wasn't for us, you'd be dead by
now and you wouldn't have died easy or nice. Them were mean
bastards, the meanest they come."

"And you?"

"Us? All you can have against us, friend, is we don't want to do
anything'll hurt you. We won't even let you hurt yourself."

"You're not cops."

"Friend, we're going to pretend like you never said that. We just
want to think you don't know no better. You ain't meant to be in-
sulting."

The car came off the paved road onto what sounded like gravel.
After a few more twists and turns it came to a stop. The man who

had been riding beside me left the car. From a count of door slams I concluded that the driver had also come out from behind the wheel. I was alone in the car. My legs and feet were back to feeling they belonged to me and they were unbound.

The temptation to make a quick jump out of the car and run for it was overwhelming. Whatever I had left to me at that moment that was capable of rational thought was telling me I could never make it. It was in every way impossible. Running blind, I would inevitably stray off the driveway and, within even a very few steps, I would be hopelessly lost and all too easily recaptured. There was no way I could free my hands and therefore no way I could rip off the blindfold. Also there was almost no likelihood that I could be given the time for so much as beginning to work at it.

So why did I try it? Pride? Some feeling that it was shameful to do nothing, to go along meekly, lamb to the slaughter stuff? There certainly was some of that, but for the most part it was desperation. Desperation is like that. It's the rejection of all reason.

I jumped and I made the lousiest possible job of it. I don't believe my trouble just then was only not seeing. It was that I was doing it without arm freedom. I suppose an armless man might with time train himself to balance without an arm swing. I don't know. Be that as it may, I was attempting it totally unpracticed in any such esoteric athleticism.

My landing was hopelessly unstable. I strained every muscle, trying for that instinctive arm waving you do in an attempt to achieve balance. My arms, bound down to my sides, were, of course, out of action. They just strained against the strap and I toppled forward, landing face down in the gravel. Since I couldn't bring my hands up to brake my fall, my arms were again reduced to straining futilely against the strap while my face hit the gravel with only the bulk of my blindfold to cushion the impact.

Quickly more hands than I could at the moment count were grabbing hold of me and setting me back on my feet. They expostulated with me and as before it was all kindness and concern interspersed with gentle and indulgent scolding. I could differentiate three voices and none of them was either of my pair of rescuers. I had been delivered into other hands.

They were telling me that I should be more careful. There was no need to hurry. I shouldn't attempt anything without waiting to be helped. That's what they were there for. They would look after me and they would help me. I shouldn't be trying to do anything for myself. I should leave everything to them. After all, I should have recognized by now that I was in good hands.

"You mustn't be foolish. You should just see what you've done to yourself now. We're going to have to clean the cuts and get them to stop bleeding. And why? Just because you were impatient."

I was getting the hands sorted out, matching them to my count of the voices. I had a man on either side of me. They had their hands on me, ostensibly holding me steady while a third man mopped at my stinging face. The words and the tone indicated that they were supporting hands. On the feel of them, as they gripped my arms, I knew that they were there not for support but for restraint.

The third man came away from ministering to my face. The two who were holding me began moving me along. Although it was obvious that there was nothing effective I could do about it, I was, nevertheless determined to do what I could. I had too long permitted myself to be fooled, too long charmed into submission. Now I would have to be forced every step of the way. I was not going to go along docilely. I kicked and struggled in their grasp.

This new crew hadn't the discipline or possibly the patience of the pair they had replaced. The third man had come around behind me and spoke from in back. All that sweet concern was now gone out of his voice.

"Stop that shit," he said. "You'll stop it quick if you know what's good for you."

The other two considered that inadequate.

"Don't talk to him," one of them said. "Just belt him one."

The other lug had a more specific approach. "Kick his ass for him," he said.

The man behind me had his own method. With one hand he grabbed a firm hold on my belt. What had been a relatively humane, even if effective, way of binding my arms now became agonizingly constricting. The blood flow was again going to be cut off from my hands. With his other hand he tried to grab a solid hand-

ful of the seat of my pants. Finding not enough slack to afford him
a good grip there, he reached lower to fasten on an area which
afforded him the double accomplishment of achieving a firm grip
and subjecting me to agony so bone-dissolving that it drained all
the fight out of me.

Holding me that way, the three of them lifted just enough to
keep me suspended with my feet only barely touching the ground.
In this way they moved me indoors. Whether it was carrying or
frog-marching is not easily said.

For the rest of it, that was the way they handled it. The three of
them worked on me together. Whatever they did, they did roughly.
Most of the roughness, I suppose, could be called necessary since
all along I was trying to fight them. Again and again, however,
there were those moments that went beyond the necessary to slip in
the touch of agony. Every one of those moments of excess, furthermore, was done with deliberate calculation and expert skill. They
adhered too neatly to prescribed limits. If it had been impulsive
savagery, they would have slipped at least once. They would have
done something that would have left a mark.

When they had me stripped, a fourth man took over. His was a
new voice, markedly different from any I had been hearing since I
had been first kidnapped. To varying degrees, the others all had
something of the sound of the street. This was cultivated—not pre-
tentiously so, possibly noticeable only in contrast to what I had
been hearing all through this time I had been so excessively dependent on hearing. Other times I might have taken his sure-footed
grammar for granted. Under the circumstances it was arresting.

"Mr. Bagby," he said, "if you will just settle down for a minute
or two, nobody will touch you. All I want to do is help you."

"Please," I said, "I've had more than I can take of that garbage."

"Just hear me out. You can't think that you don't need help. Your
face is a chopped-up mess. It's nothing serious. At least, it doesn't
have to be serious. It's just a lot of small cuts from the gravel. If
they are cleaned, they will heal without any problems, but you
can't just leave them with the dirt ground into them."

"You want to help me," I said. "You're concerned about my
chopped-up face. Just drive to the nearest hospital, leave me on the

hospital steps, and drive away. I promise you, I'll count to a thousand before I go in."

He chuckled. "Like an overgrown foundling, Mr. Bagby?" he said. "I haven't the authority to do that."

"Then go away and don't bother me."

"I can't do that either, and I wouldn't if I could. I'd hate myself if I did. So one question. With those dirty cuts it's important. When did you last have anti-tetanus immunization?"

That did it. Nobody got to say any more until my three keepers got me down again and were keeping me down.

"You're not giving me any shot," I said.

"Certainly not if you don't need it."

"I don't need it. I keep my anti-tetanus up. I always have."

"Great. Everyone should. Too many people don't. You're all right there then. We'll try it this way. First thing I'll deal with the cuts. I know you're impatient to have the blindfold off, but that's only an annoyance. The cuts come first."

"Blindfold first," I said. "Maybe I'll manage to trust you if I can see your face. The cuts can wait that long."

"No, Mr. Bagby. They've waited too long already. If you won't hold still while I'm dealing with them, the boys can hold you still. I'd rather it wouldn't be necessary, but I can do it either way."

"I'm not holding still for anything."

"Your choice, Mr. Bagby," he said. If the sound of regret was counterfeit, the guy was a great dissembler. He switched quickly to a tone of command. "All right, men," he said. "Two of you will hold him down and one will hold his head steady. Think you can handle it or will you need help?"

I wondered whether the manpower was unlimited or if he was trying to impress on me the futility of struggle. If so, he was undertaking the impossible. By that time I was dedicated to futility.

They held me as directed and he went to work. He had great hands. He worked deftly and rapidly. I became so bemused with wondering about the guy that, without realizing it, I lost track of my determination to struggle. He, of course, noticed it.

"He's all right now, fellows," he said. "You can let him go."

That brought me back from my wandering. I wasn't going to be that easily seduced. They had to take fresh holds on me.

"You can't trust him a minute," one of them said. "The onliest way you can do with him is you learn him a good hard lesson."

"Watch it, my friend." The man paused long enough to offer the warning. "You're the one who can be taught a lesson you'll never forget, and it'll be because you won't be living long enough for forgetting anything."

Nothing more was said until he had finished the patch job on the facial cuts and he made a fresh stab at reasoning with me.

"I'd like you to simmer down long enough to listen to me," he said. "You'll want to pay close attention to what I'll be telling you. You go on thrashing about that way and you won't be paying attention. You're not stupid. You know by now that fighting the boys is useless. You can't do yourself any good that way."

He explained that he had taken care of the cuts on my face. That much of the job was done and that much of it had been manageable even though I'd been fighting it.

"You slowed me up a little," he said, "but that was all."

The tapes that had bound my ankles had been wound on over my socks and they had been taken away with my socks. They were being removed. They were no problem, nor were the ones that had been applied to cloth at my elbows and my knees. There were, however, these others, firmly stuck to skin and hair.

"I want to take those off without hurting you," he said, "and certainly without ripping off strips of skin. I have a solvent that will do it."

He explained that his solvent was effective but that, using it, he would have to work rapidly. He could leave the stuff on my skin for only the shortest possible time. It was a powerful irritant. It had to be applied quickly and quickly washed away. To handle the tape on my wrists nothing would be required but speed in applying the solvent and in washing it away. Working on my head, however, he was going to have to be most careful.

"If even a drop of it gets into your mouth or up your nose," he said, "you'll have a most painful and difficult time. If it gets into your eyes, we'll be in really bad trouble and it's there, on your face and head, that the solvent is most needed. It was tough enough to begin with, but you did make it worse with all the little cuts on your face. I have to keep the stuff out of those as well."

What it came to was that the speed and care the job required would not be possible unless I cooperated and held absolutely still. It wouldn't matter how many assistants he might enlist for the task of holding me down. They couldn't guarantee him the complete immobility he required.

"That I must have from you," he said, "and I expect that you'll give it to me. You do want the blindfold off and that should be enough reason for you to cooperate."

He told me I had a choice. It would either be cooperation or I would force him to resort to his only possible alternative which would be to give me a shot that would put me out completely and keep me under until he had finished his work.

"That," I said, "is no choice at all."

"I'm glad you see it that way," he said. "I have the needle right here. I much prefer not to use it."

"You're not giving me any shot," I said.

He told the goons to let go of me. "We'll see how well he does on his own," he said.

I was very good at it. Pride had carried me as far as it could go. The time had come for surrender. He waited for a few moments and then warned me that he was about to begin.

"I can well imagine," he said, "that what you most want is to have the blindfold off. We'll start with that. So now be absolutely still. For this bit, it's your eyesight."

Perhaps he shouldn't have said that last. It brought on the thought that I was trusting this guy and not because I had any very good reason for this trust but only because I had no choice. I was all too well aware that what would happen to me would happen, no matter what I did or tried to do. The choice I had been offered would in no way have affected what he would be doing, only the degree to which I might have any knowledge of what was happening to me.

There were two things that kept me from collapsing into complete panic. I concentrated on those. One was the feel I had of the way he was working. The speed of it was taking nothing away from its deftness and precision. The other thing was the prospect of being able to see again. The anticipation was overwhelming, even while the questions it provoked seemed hopelessly baffling.

If I was to be permitted to see, then all my assumptions about my situation needed radical revision. But how to revise them? I could form no picture that would even begin to make any kind of sense that I didn't very much want to reject. I was swinging back to thinking the good-guy-bad-guy routine. All this great care and kind solicitude would be part of the softening-up process. I would be sucked into doing for the good guys what I might not do for the bad guys.

They might be hoping that they could win my trust, and a big move toward winning it would be permitting me to see their faces. If that didn't suffice for drawing from me what they wanted, there would then be the threat of turning me over to the bad guys. There was a corollary to it, however, and from that I was trying to steer my mind away. There could be only one condition under which these people would permit me to see their faces and that would be that I was never to come out of their hands alive.

You might think that a sensible man, once he'd had that thought, would lose all his appetite for seeing; but would you expect a blind man, given the promise of sight, to be sensible? I was afraid to look and I couldn't help looking.

The blindfold came off and automatically my eyes opened. As quickly they closed again. They had opened into a blinding glare of light. It felt as though its intensity seared my eyeballs. My extraordinary ministering angel was immediately sympathetic and abjectly apologetic.

"Oh, sorry," he said. "Stupid of me. Of course, the light hurts your eyes. It would anyone's, and after the long time yours have been covered, it would be much worse."

I forced my eyes open. I had to try for anything I might see beyond the glare. I had almost no time and I saw almost nothing. The light was too much. My eyes couldn't adjust to it. Then there wasn't even that. He shielded my eyes by laying a damp cool towel over

them. So I'd seen that much, the towel coming down and the hands
that held it. They were the hands of a black man.

I thanked him for the towel. "But," I said, "I'd rather you took
the light away."

"Of course, you would. It won't be much longer now. There's
only the one more lot of tape to go. There's much of that. It's the
stuff that was holding your gag in place. I'll need the light for it,
but hold still and I'll have it off in no time. As soon as I'm through,
we'll take the light away."

That seemed reasonable enough.

"I can wait that long," I said.

"Good man. Now very still. I don't want to get any of this mean
stuff in your mouth."

He was as good as his word, but only that good and no more. He
didn't go an inch beyond the precise limits of what he had
promised.

One of the men—he had been sitting perched on the bed beside
me during the time when they had been holding me down—hadn't
moved. Even after I'd agreed to hold still for the tape removal, he
had remained sitting with his weight leaned lightly against me and
his arm arched over my body. Although he wasn't holding me anymore, he was just enough in contact to keep me aware that he was
in position to make the quick grab and hold me down if I should
make even the first move toward trying to get up off the bed. That
lug wasn't leaving me.

The job was quickly finished and, only moments after the deft
fingers came away from my face, my eyes were uncovered. The
light, as promised, had been shifted off me. Its beam was now
turned down on a table that stood beside the bed. Apart from the
brightly lighted table top, the room was totally dark. I could see
nothing.

Just for the joy of seeing, I looked hard at what I could see. I saw
the black man's hands and forearms and the stuff he had laid out
on the table. He was stowing it in a small bag. There were several
small bottles of liquid, Band-Aids in various sizes, tweezers, gauze
pads, and a hypodermic syringe complete with needle.

"I'd like to thank you," I said, "but I prefer to see a man face to face when I'm thanking him."

"There's no need to thank me. I just do my job."

"Then I don't see your face?"

"I'm a modest man. I don't like showing my face."

"Then you don't trust me?"

"I can't expect more of you than I would expect of myself in a like situation, and I do have a high opinion of myself."

"I'd like to speak plainly," I said. "Whether I am still being held by my kidnappers or am now in the hands of men who hijacked me from the kidnappers I don't know. Either way I'm a prisoner. I am being held against my will. Oughtn't I be told why and what is to be done before I'll be released?"

"Sorry, Mr. Bagby. It's not my department. I can only assume that priority was given to tending to your medical needs, and I would say properly. That's only a guess. I follow orders. I have no voice in policy."

It was all the answer I had from him. He had cleared all his stuff into his bag and had snapped the bag shut. He turned off the lamp. Lighting his way with a flashlight, he went out the door and shut it behind him. Since the bed I was on was set against a wall and his flashlight had permitted me to follow his progress to the door in the opposite wall but nothing more, I had learned one thing. I was being held in what was probably a small room. I knew of a certainty that it was small in at least that one dimension.

I was not alone. I knew I still had the one man with me. He hadn't moved from his perch beside me on the bed. In the total darkness of that room there might have been others. I had no way of knowing. I was listening for a rustle of movement or the sound of breathing. I could hear nothing.

The room wasn't stuffy. I could feel a current of comfortably cool air pass across my naked body. It was not steady. It came and went. Listening hard, I detected the softest of humming sounds during the times when I was feeling it. They seemed to turn off when it died down. I figured it for an air-conditioner operating on a thermostat rather than an open window and an intermittent breeze. There was also the blackness. Nights are rarely that dark, and surely there had been time and enough for dawn to have come up if not even full daylight.

"What time is it?" I asked.

"You thinking of going some place?"

"Buck naked?"

"Yeah and taking rifle slugs up your ass every step of the way."

There seemed little purpose in continuing that conversation, but the goon had uncorked.

"How do you like that uppity nigger?" he said. "One of these times he's going to get me mad enough. I'll belt him in the mouth and, when I do, I'll slug him so hard he'll have his teeth coming out his asshole."

"What is he? A doctor or something?"

"He's a goddamn nigger. Shit, man, didn't you smell it on him?"

Leaning over me the way he was, he had for some time been assaulting me with his odor of stale sweat. Much as I would have liked to remark on it, I found myself speculating instead on whether, if I went along with him by pretending a shared prejudice, I could establish some sort of rapport with the lug. I am inclined to think it was simple good sense as much as my revulsion against doing it that stopped me from the attempt.

In any event, there would have been no time. The door opened and three men came in, shutting the door behind them. I could make the count because there were three flashlights with which they lighted their way. I thought it would be the same company reassembling, but when one of them spoke, it was again a new voice, one I hadn't heard before.

I placed it at a level somewhere between the street speech of the strong-arm types and the cultivated language of the black. It was correct speech, but with a gutter undertone to it. In any case, it was the voice of authority. The man gave orders and he was obeyed. None of the others spoke at all.

Beaming his flashlight at a spot on the floor a few feet away from the bed, he ordered a chair to be set just there. A chair was moved out of the dark and put where his light beam indicated. Then that glaring lamp was turned on with its light focused on the chair.

Evidently satisfied with this furniture arrangement, he turned his flashlight beam on me.

"Mr. Bagby," he said, "will you please come and sit in the chair?"

It was too much. "When they do this in the movies," I said, "they allow the man to have his clothes on, or are you aiming for an X-rating?"

He responded to that by addressing not me but my keeper.

"Bring him over and sit him down," he said.

It was an order delivered with the most insolent parade-ground snap. I had to fight that. I knew I couldn't win. Three against one, the odds were overwhelming. I would have known that much even if I hadn't had all that previous demonstration of it.

The man who had been guarding me made the quick grab and for the moments while the others were closing in he held me down. By the movement of their flashlight beams I could see them coming, but that was all they were giving me. In the light of the lamp I could see the chair and only the chair. The flashlights, except when shining on me they gave me a glimpse of the hands of the lug who was holding me, illuminated nothing but portions of the floor. It looked like concrete. For what it was worth I could conclude I was in a cellar. It was all painstakingly careful. I was seeing nothing I could later identify.

The coordination was so remarkable that I had to think they were carrying out a process that was something like their daily routine, or that otherwise it had been long rehearsed. They were on top of me when they switched off their flashlights. They needed their hands for coping with me and they were taking no chances that in any possible flailing around a stray beam might flip up to reveal one of their faces.

At the same moment the guy who was giving the orders switched his flash on, swept the beam across the floor to the bed and raised it just enough to put the light on me. They would be having light for what they were to do, but I was to be afforded sight of nothing more than hands and forearms.

Suddenly I came down with the idea that my struggling might be to some purpose. If I did it in short spurts with intervals between when it would seem that I was gathering my strength for another explosive effort, during such intervals I could be giving my all to seeing whatever the head man's flash might be revealing to me.

I tried it and, for what it was worth, I did see. It had been only a small hope and it came to virtually nothing. I saw hands and forearms. I had hoped for at least one distinguishing mark. A missing finger or part of a finger might have been too much to hope for, but tattoos had seemed a possibility. So there were tattoos, but they couldn't have been more unimaginatively ordinary. A pair of linked hearts on one forearm without even a name to individualize them and the inevitable nude babe on another. Universal commonplaces of the tattoo artist's pattern book, as an identifying feature they would count for little more than brown hair or blue eyes. Men by the thousands are similarly ornamented.

If I had not been involved in this all-but-futile effort to see something it would be useful to remember, I could probably have made their job a little more difficult for them, but the end result would have been no different. They planted me in the chair and held me pinned to it. The lamp was raised to beam full in my face. The questioning began.

"What do you know about Lansing Monroe?"

"He's dead."

"You can do better than that."

"He was machine-gunned. That means he was murdered. Suicide is possible with a handgun. It can even be done with a shotgun or a rifle. With a machine gun it's impossible and so is accidental death. So it was murder. Did you need me to tell you that?"

CHAPTER 11

My inquisitor switched to reasoning with me.

"Mr. Bagby," he said, "you are very good at playing the fool. You may have the time for it. I don't. I'm a busy man. The sooner you tell me what we need to know, the sooner we can let you go home. You are not a fool and you are not an innocent. You have been closely associated with Inspector Schmidt for too long a time to expect anyone to believe that you don't know the ropes."

With that preamble he told me what I knew. They were doing this the hard way. There was that most useful drug they could inject into me. It would have me babbling.

"That," he said, "is the civilized way of doing it. These boys here are not civilized. They have another way they much prefer. They have a great repertoire of exquisitely sadistic tricks. Since it is obvious that you don't appreciate the fact that we have been very good to you or even that you owe it to us that you are still alive and not gone the way of your old friend, Lansing Monroe, we are not fools enough to think we can count on your gratitude."

In my interest, and he stressed the fact that it had been done very much in my interest, they had killed two men. He and I knew that the killing had been a contribution to the public peace and tranquility, but the state of New Jersey would be calling it murder.

"We could have called the cops and put them on the trail," he said. "They could have chased the car and maybe even rescued you. We had our reasons for taking the law into our own hands, but we cannot expect the state to recognize the legitimacy of our reasons."

Far more to my advantage than to theirs they had put themselves in a difficult and even dangerous position. He wasn't going to try to tell me that it had been done out of pure altruism. They considered themselves entitled to have something out of all they had done for me and they were going to have it, whatever it would take to get it. I had information they needed and I would be giving it to them.

"We know that as soon as we turn you loose," he said, "you'll be straight on to the police with the complete story of everything that's happened to you. We can't hope that you won't be giving them everything you can that might lead them to us. That's why we can't let you see any of us. It will be better for everyone if there is nobody you can describe or pick out of a lineup."

He told me that up to that point they had been treating me well and that they would like to go on treating me well. He offered me various reasons for it. They were not savages. They had nothing against me. They were, however, cautious men. If in spite of all their careful precautions there might have been a slipup somewhere and their part in the night's events could be traced to them, they were hoping that it would be counted in their favor if there was every evidence that they had dealt kindly and well with me. They had not drugged me. They had not tortured me.

"If worse comes to worst, of course," he said, "and you force me to turn the boys loose to have their fun with you, it will reverse the situation. There will then be no possibility that we could ever turn you loose. You get my meaning, I hope."

I got his meaning. I could have questioned the reasonableness of it since he had himself brought up the possibility of the tongue-loosening shot, but the matter was clearly not up for discussion.

"Your meaning is clear enough," I said.

"Good. Then let's get down to it so we can finish our business quickly and get you home."

"What do you want?"

"Where was Monroe getting his cocaine?"

"Was he getting it? If he was, I didn't know."

"You were friends."

"He was the kind of man who called everyone a friend. Maybe it was that he had a warm, outgoing nature, and I haven't. I knew the man. He may have thought me a friend. I never thought of him that way."

"That's pretty snotty."

"No. It was no more than the difference in the way we each of us defined the word 'friend.'"

A voice spoke from just behind my ear.

"He's stalling. Leave me soften him up a little and try again."

My questioner was having none of that. "If I want anything from you, I'll tell you," he said. "Till then, shut up." He returned to me. "Go on, Mr. Bagby," he said.

"We belonged to the same club. He played a creditable game of squash. There were times in the course of club tournaments when it worked out that I was matched against him. So you can say we were that friendly. Squash, the way we play it, is a friendly game. But Monroe and I never set it up to play a game on our own. It was only when the tournament schedule would happen to bring us together. Otherwise, I'd run into him in the club locker room or at the club bar. That was how much I knew him."

"You never snorted with him?"

"If he did, he did it with other people or alone, not with me."

"Never talked to you about it?"

"Look. Even if he used to speak of me as his friend, it was just a way of speaking. Whatever there was between us was too casual for him to have confided in me. A man doesn't confide in someone he knows that slightly, and more than anyone else, he wouldn't in me."

"Why so specially not in you?"

"You named it yourself—the long time I've been close to Inspector Schmidt," I said. "You can't think that you are alone in being aware of that association. Why would he be trusting me not to be turning him in to the Narcs?"

"Member of the same club? Blood brothers?"

"Not that kind of a club."

He switched away from that line of questioning. I hoped I had satisfied him in that area.

"After the funeral," he said, "that same night, you had somebody in your apartment. He ripped the whole place apart. What did he take?"

"He ripped everything apart and dumped everything out on the floor—books, papers, clothes, groceries, you name it—it's all there piled up on the floor, everything mixed up together. I won't know what he took till I have it sorted out and back where it belongs, and so far I've only begun on making the smallest dent in doing that."

I didn't think it was necessary to tell him that I was fairly certain it had been a burglar who had taken nothing.

"You have a burglary. You come home and find the place all torn up. You have things that are valuable and things that perhaps don't have much value but they mean a lot to you for one reason or another. You'd hate to lose them. You go looking for them first thing. Didn't you do that?"

"As far as I could manage to look for anything in that jumbled mass," I said, "I tried. Things burglars usually go for—typewriter, camera, TV, hifi—they were all there. Nothing of that was taken. I don't go for jewelry and the little I have, watch and cuff links, I had on me. I use checks and credit cards. I only have a little cash and I carry that on me. I never leave any stashed around the house."

"Ripping the place apart the way he did, he was looking for something. Did he get it?"

"No."

"What was it?"

"I have no possible way of knowing that."

"Come on, Mr. Bagby. I thought we were doing fine. If you know he didn't get it, then you still have it. So you know what it is."

"No," I said, "I'm figuring it from the places he looked. I know I had nothing in those places. So it follows that he found nothing."

I ran through my catalogue of damage. "He wrecked all that," I said, "looking for whatever it was he thought I had. Since I never had anything I could have hidden in any of those places and since I never opened any of them up to hide anything inside them, I'm just making the reasonable assumption that he couldn't have found anything where there had been nothing to be found."

"You're too smart to have kept it in the apartment. Safe deposit box?"

"I've never had a safe deposit box. I've never had anything to put in one."

"You were kidnapped last night. Why?"

It seemed a stupid question but the "last night" caught my attention. That was a crumb of information. As I had been guessing, the night was over. We were into the next day. I tried for more.

"Does the prisoner get breakfast?" I asked. "If it's getting on toward lunch time, I'll settle for brunch."

"As soon as I have finished with you," he said, "there will be breakfast if you want it. We've been thinking you wouldn't want to stop for it. You'd rather get back home that much sooner. You were going to tell me why you were kidnapped."

"Was I hoping for too much when I thought you might tell me? I can only guess that their reason for putting the grab on me was the same as yours is for holding me all this time after you'd hijacked me away from them. They must have wanted to ask me these same unanswerable questions. If it's to be a matter of guessing, I'd say you are in a position to make far better guesses than I can. You know who they were. I don't even know that."

"Then let's go back to Lansing Monroe. Who was close to him? I'm thinking a real friend, a man he might have snorted with. People like him, it's a social thing for them. It's like drinking. If they do it alone, it will be only some of the time. Most of the time it's social."

I was being invited to submit a list of candidates for kidnapping. I was happy with the thought that I could make an honest answer without giving these fiendish smoothies anything. I just had to hope I might be believed.

"I'm sorry. I just didn't know him well enough for that. As I told you, he was one of those hail-fellow-well-met types who come on superfriendly with everybody from the Moonie passing out tracts at the corner and the club bootblack to the oldest member who was once chairman of the Stock Exchange or something equally eminent. It could have been anyone or no one. I just have no way of knowing."

"People seem to think that you and Monroe were real close."

"What people?"

"At the funeral, the crazy old guy, the uncle."

"You said it." I picked up on his words. "The problem seems to be too many crazy young guys who are setting too much store by the insane babblings of that crazy old guy."

"You're saying the old man just made it up?"

"I'm saying that Lansing Monroe might very well have done some idle talking about his friend George Bagby who was just about at the right hand of Inspector Schmidt. I can well imagine that Monroe might have talked like that and that the old man would have taken off from there. Pass any bit of nonsense from nut to nut and it grows."

"Very well, Mr. Bagby," he said, as he switched the lamp off. I'd had my eyes shut against the glare of it, but it had been a red glow through my closed eyelids. "I had hoped you could tell us much more; but what you don't know you don't know. You'll be out of here and on your way home in a very few minutes now."

"Can't be too soon," I said.

"Then you don't want to stop for breakfast?"

"I don't want to stop for anything."

I had opened my eyes. Again it was the blackness punctuated only by the glow of four flashlights. They were moving toward the door and the four of them were going in a body. I couldn't see any of them. I could estimate their movements by the four pools of light that blended and separated where they spread over the floor. I jumped up from the chair and moved to join them. Misjudging the distance, I bumped into someone's back. A hand planted on my chest shoved me backward to sit down hard on the rough concrete of the floor.

"You will want to stop for your clothes, Mr. Bagby," the man said. "For your pants, if for nothing more."

With that they were out the door and shutting it after them. I pulled to my feet and headed in that direction as best I could remember it. I strayed off course a bit, but feeling along the wall, I found the door. It was locked. Coming away from the locked door, I found myself badly disoriented.

I couldn't content myself with just standing and waiting in the dark, but I could think of no alternative I liked better. I had to settle for leaning against the wall. I had come up with a new thought I could worry. I would be going home in short order. That sounded great but only as long as I could avoid questioning what might have been meant by that word "home." Would it be my messed up apartment or was it a savagely witty euphemism for my last resting place?

I was to be turned loose, but it was to be done without my ever seeing anyone I could later identify. Thus far they had managed it well by making adroit use of the dark. Away from this cellar, however, it would no longer be dark. It would have been idiotic to think that they were going to take me all the way home and deposit me on my doorstep. They would be taking me out of this cellar and driving me away from this place to some spot where they could drop me with absolute assurance that I would not be able to lead the police right back to them.

For that it would have to be another blindfold. It was pretty much a certainty that they had me in a place so isolated that they could be safe in moving me from house to car with no worry of some chance passerby taking notice of a blindfolded man. I could imagine that part of it being manageable for them. What troubled me was how they could ever manage a place where I could be safely dropped off.

It couldn't be anywhere along the country road that led to this hideaway of theirs. It would be too easy for the police to track back along the road. It would need to be off somewhere on an isolated stretch of some other road that would offer no clue to where I had been.

The question I was confronting had to do with how they could manage in between. If they were to be offering no retraceable trail, it seemed to me that they would have to be taking a route that would bring them through at least one town. How were they going to drive through the traffic of some busy town in daylight with a gagged and blindfolded passenger?

I could think of no way. I could only hope that for this kind of game their minds were better equipped than mine. I'd had too much experience of them to believe even for a moment that they wouldn't have prepared a safe way of handling the problem. If they hadn't, it was not going to mean that just to send me home they were ready to put themselves to even the slightest risk. It would mean that they had settled for a way that would be safe for them even though not for me, that for me home was to be one variety or the other of the hereafter. I'm afraid I was reduced to standing there in the dark and urging God to make the bastards into intellectual giants.

They came and it was four of them. As before, I had the flashlight count. This time, when the head man spoke, it wasn't a new voice. I had an immediate recognition. It was again the black.

"Mr. Bagby," he said, "you are going to have to put up with some more discomfort. I'm sorry. If there could be any way that would be easier on you, I would go to any amount of trouble to do it, but there just is no other way. I am not going to pretend that it won't be uncomfortable, particularly psychologically. The psychological discomfort will far exceed the physical, but that's all it will be—just discomfort. If you concentrate on thinking that with every minute of it that passes, you will be one minute closer to being back in circulation again, you'll be fine."

I thought I had the answer. It seemed so simple that I almost laughed, considering the absurdity of my not having thought of it at once. It wasn't as though they hadn't already used the device. When they'd been bringing me in, they'd explained the way I looked to the satisfaction of the toll taker by telling him that they were taking me where my injuries could be dealt with.

This guy, with his skills, could easily do a fresh blindfold that would look like a surgical dressing. A man who'd had eye surgery was being taken to the doctor for a post-operative check. It made sense except that I was wrong again.

As he gave me full preparation for what was to come by describing in detail what they were about to do, I realized that I had been considering only one of their hazards. They overlooked nothing. They would be guaranteeing themselves against every possible danger.

They had prepared a box large enough to hold me. They were

going to put me in it and carry it out to a panel truck. He assured me that the box was perforated with adequate air holes. There would be no danger of suffocation. It would be cramped quarters and I would have to endure that for the ride to a place in the woods where they could leave the box.

"The box," he said, "will be locked."

He was telling me this as though he were proposing something completely reasonable. I was breaking out in a sweat. It felt as though I were sweating ice cubes.

"The important thing is not to panic," he said. "The lock is on a time device. The lock will release exactly five minutes after we set the box down in the woods. The thing you should do is stay quiet and wait. There's a bell. It's nothing fancy, it's just like an alarm clock. When you hear the bell, you just push on the lid and that's it. You'll be out of there."

"I'll never be in there," I said. "No way."

"You have no choice, Mr. Bagby. We can't just go on keeping you indefinitely. We can't afford to do that. You won't be so deep in the wood that you'll have any trouble finding your way out to the wood road. You can't go wrong there because if you take it in the wrong direction, you'll know it before you've gone a hundred yards. The road dead ends."

"No," I said. "I can't trust it. How can I trust you?"

"You can trust me because when you trusted me before, you had no reason to regret it."

"No. It's like being buried alive."

That is what I said. It wasn't quite what I was thinking. They were about to bury me alive and this smoothie was trying to talk me into going gladly into my coffin.

"I'm sorry," he said. "Believe me, Mr. Bagby. This isn't the way I wanted to do it."

I thought he was still talking about my coffin. Three of the four flashlights that had been playing on me snapped off. Only the one remained. Two of the strong-arm lugs fastened on me and held me. I felt the four hands on me and I could see them in the pool of light. I was putting everything I had into trying to break free; but when I saw the black's hands move into the light with the syringe and the needle, from somewhere I came up with strength I'd never known before. I flailed about. I may have broken away from some of the grips they had on me. More likely they let go of those to gang up on the one arm. They were ignoring the rest of me while they held that steady. I felt the cold of the alcohol swab.

"On the point of burying a man alive," I asked myself, "do you concern yourself about protecting him from needle infection?"

It may be that I do remember thinking that a crazy perfectionist could just be following habitual procedure. I do remember feeling the needle go in and then there was nothing. It's been my guess that it was a Valium shot. Maybe you've never been given one. Its effect is quick and sudden. You have not even a momentary awareness of going under, and you come out of it in the same way. There is not even the briefest interval of fuzziness or of groping your way back to consciousness. You just go out and come back in with absolutely no knowledge of anything in between.

I had only the one way of knowing I had been unconscious. I was no longer struggling in anybody's grasp. Nobody was talking to me. I was alone. I was no longer upright or erect. I was still in total darkness, but now I was lying on my side, all folded together so that I was occupying the minimum of space. That stock question—where am I?—never came into my mind. I knew where I was.

I was absolutely clear on everything that had come before the unconsciousness. I was locked in that box. My mind shuddered away from letting itself think coffin, but the thought was there and it was making my heart pound. I was in motion. I could feel the vibration and an occasional slight bump. I felt no side-to-side jostling. That would mean I had been out long enough to have been loaded into the box, moved to the truck, and driven far enough to be off the winding country road and on the straight run of the highway.

In the constriction of the box I could hardly move at all. My arms were pressed against my body. I could move them back and forth but only something less than an inch. Where they were touching ribs and thighs and calves, however, I could tell even from the slight rub that I was still naked. It was bare skin against bare skin. They hadn't stopped to put any clothes on me.

Images hung in my mind—men in the white shirt and black suit laid out in their coffins. I wasn't laid out and there was no white shirt or correct black suit. I sheered away from exploring the thought of what might be *de rigueur* for burying a man alive. It was important that I shouldn't panic. The man had said that.

There were air holes. There was no possibility of suffocation. I took a deep breath. The box did seem fairly well ventilated. I could believe that there were air holes. Surely there wouldn't be air holes if this was to be my coffin. Why would it matter to them—or, for that matter, to me—whether I died of suffocation below ground or above?

I worked at keeping my thoughts concentrated on my breathing. I couldn't call the air fresh, but each breath seemed to be as good as the one before. I could tell myself that my breathing was not depleting the oxygen. That I was obviously off on a long ride should hardly have been worth thinking about. Certainly it couldn't have been otherwise. Whatever they would be doing with me at the end of it, they would certainly not want it to be on their doorstep or in any spot that could offer a lead to the place where they had been holding me.

All the nerves in my body, all my bones and muscles were clamoring for it to be over. Every thought in my head was dreading the moment. I was working hard at thinking that it would be no more than the end of the ride and the end of my confinement, but it was a thought that I just couldn't keep with me. The one thought was always there, and from every effort I made to push it off it bounced back and again filled my mind. The end of this ride was going to be the end of everything.

I had not even a moment of doubt about when we left the highway. I knew it immediately. There was the change in the vibration rate. It was a shift to a slightly rougher road surface. Then quickly there began the side-to-side sway and a heavily increased jolting. That would be a country road and one that was poorly maintained. It had holes in it.

Trying to disregard the thought that was saying, "Much good it can do you," I concentrated on recognizing and remembering. It had been highway but not turnpike. We had come off it on a simple turn. There had been no long curve of an exit ramp and no pause for a tollbooth. I couldn't have been wrong about those two items. I had been waiting for them, counting on sensing them when they would come, bracing myself for making a try at screaming in the hope that I might be heard by a tollbooth attendant. There had been no exit ramp and no tollbooth. I couldn't have missed them.

What had been cramped discomfort growing into pain had now, with the swinging and jolting, become pain growing into agony. I was beginning to think it was coming to the place where I could be wanting nothing but the end—any end. Then it stopped and I could only wish that it would begin again. I wasn't ready to die.

It was only moments, however, before I had something else to think about. I was seeing light. At first it was only faint light, but with a new kind of movement and a new sound—a scraping sound— the light brightened. At the same time there was a marked change in the air. It freshened. I could work that out. My box did have air holes. It was being pulled out of the stuffiness and the dark of the closed truck into daylight and fresh air.

Quickly I was again being bumped about but this, too, was different. The box was being carried and nobody was being over-careful to hold it steady. Fresh country smells came in through the air holes. I thought of leaf mold and the pitchy scent of pine. I dragged in deep breaths and tried to remember when breathing had last been so good.

The light coming through the air holes kept flickering. I recognized that for leaf shadow. I concentrated on the light. When with the last bump—and a big one—the movement stopped, the flickering light remained. I had never been so grateful for light. Just then it meant everything. The box had been dumped on the ground. It hadn't been dumped into a hole.

There was the disquieting thought that this might be only for a time while they would be digging the hole, but I didn't have too much trouble ridding myself of that one. I'd had too much experience with these bastards. It wouldn't be the way they operated. If there was to be a grave, they would have had it ready dug before bringing me here.

I lay scrunched up in the box, staring at the light and listening hard. No one was saying anything. I heard what might have been the snapping of twigs. Then I heard doors slam and diminishing sound I took to be the truck driving away. After that it was nothing. Only gradually did it come to me that there was something. There was the steady ticking.

The man had said five minutes before I would hear the bell and the lock would release. I started counting seconds. Three hundred seconds would do it but you mustn't count fast. It will be unreliable because anxiety will push you into rushing the count. And what makes you so sure their crazy gadget will work? Suppose it malfunctions and you're stuck in here? It won't malfunction. These babies are too good. They have everything under control. Other people make mistakes. They don't.

So okay. They're great, but were they leveling with you? Here you are happy as a clam, listening to that ticking. They said a clockwork mechanism and that's what it is. It's a time device that will release the lock. It works like a time bomb and it clicks away like a time bomb.

Like? How do you know that it's only like? Because they said it's a lock release? What says it isn't a bomb and you're sucked in to waiting for it to blow you up?

It had been the world's most welcome sound and now it had become the most ominous. It was ticking away the last moments of my life. I put all my strength into heaving up and pushing against the top of the box. I couldn't budge it. I couldn't detect even the slightest give. I exhausted myself and had to stop, but I couldn't stop. I just went on and on, always more feebly.

I was wishing futilely that I weren't so tightly boxed in. If I could have moved my arms and hands, I could have felt for hinges or for the screws or bolts that would hold a lock. It was no good wishing. It was impossible, and at the same time I was having the bitter thought that it was not unlikely that the lid was nailed down and there was no lock, only the clockwork mechanism to mock me with its infernal ticking while I waited for the bomb to go off.

Thoughts like that generated fresh surges of strength. I again heaved and pushed and screamed, filling my ears so full of my own noise that I didn't hear the bell. It was only when my pushing made the lid spring open and full light flooded in on me that I quieted and heard it.

I was free, but I had enfeebled myself with my hysterical struggling. My arms and legs were locked in cramps. It was a slow and painful process getting myself unwedged from that damn box. I was packed in too close to afford me any effective leverage. I had to work my way up millimeter by millimeter. An inch at a time would have seemed like lightning-fast progress. It had to be a series of tiny changes of position till I got myself to where I could hook an arm over the edge of the box and haul myself up and out.

Painfully I managed to climb out of the box only to fall flat on a bed of pine needles. I lay there panting and, while I waited for my leg muscles to begin to show promise of being able to carry me, I contemplated my nakedness.

Everything appeared to be as I'd been told it would be. I was in a wooded area. The road couldn't be far away. The box hadn't been carried any long distance after it had been taken from the truck. I was estimating it at fifty feet or less. I had no indication of the direction in which the road would lie.

While waiting till I would be able to stand and walk, I could make my plans. I had the box to use as my fixed point. Taking off from it in a straight line for fifty paces, I could reverse and return to it if in that direction I hadn't come to the road. I would try each of the four directions in turn. One way or the other would be my way out. I couldn't be lost. Then it would be the walk to the nearest house where I would ask for the use of the telephone.

I expected that it would not be a short walk. The planning had been too good in all other details. It was not going to fall down here. They had already had more than enough time to be well away. They were going to have all the additional time anyone could have wanted before I could possibly reach that first house.

I wasn't completely naked. My watch was on my wrist. I looked at it. It was only a minute or two past eleven o'clock. That was something to think about. I could expect that in that first house I would be confronting a housewife alone. Would she be inclined to open her door to a naked man and allow him the use of her telephone? The best I could hope for would be that she might listen while I shouted at her through her closed door and she would phone the police for me. At the least I had to hope that even if she wouldn't listen, she would call the police to come and take me away.

I was wondering whether I could weave myself some kind of an improvised skirt out of leaves. I didn't have a hope of finding a fig tree, and I wasn't about to look for one. I'd be lucky if I could recognize poison ivy. I didn't want to think about a housewife who might be the type who wouldn't wait for the police. There are those living in isolated houses who, it is reported, have taken to keeping a loaded shotgun handy.

I was telling myself to worry about that when I came to it. I had a more immediate problem. I had ahead of me a long barefoot walk on a rough road. I wasn't giving any time to the hope that an early hitch might come along. I remembered I had been told the road would dead end not far beyond the place where I was to have been left. Traffic isn't heavy toward the dead end of a dead-end road. Also there was the question of what sort of motorist would be likely to stop for a bare-butt hitchhiker.

Telling myself that I was stuck with it and thinking couldn't change it any, I grabbed a hold on the side of the box and pulled myself to my feet. The time had come for testing out my legs. My legs were all right and suddenly it was the best of all possible worlds.

On the far side of the box, neatly laid out on the pine needles, were my clothes. Never in my life had they been laid out that way for me before. If I had any recognition of the way they were folded and arranged, it could only have been from some movie in which someone like Cary Grant was looked after by the Hollywood version of the perfect manservant. The slacks had been cleaned and pressed. Shirt and underwear had been laundered and I couldn't remember when I had last seen a shirt so beautifully ironed. The shoes had been impeccably shined.

It would have surprised me not at all if some latter-day Jeeves had stepped from behind a tree to hold the master's britches for the master to step into them. My first impulse was to climb quickly into slacks, socks, and shoes, tuck the rest of it under my arm and take off, but I couldn't bring myself to rumple that exquisite ironing. I stopped long enough to put everything on, telling myself that the extra minute or two wouldn't matter. My torturer-benefactors had given themselves more than enough time. They had already put themselves hopelessly beyond reach.

When I had finished dressing, there were still two small objects lying on the ground. Although they weren't mine, they had been left for me under the clothes. They were a comb and a small mirror. Those babies thought of everything.

CHAPTER 12

I came out to the road on the first try. It was as I'd expected it would be, a bumpy, rutted track through the woods. I took it in the right direction, and that could have been nothing but some kind of muscle memory I hadn't even known I had. When they had unloaded me from the truck and turned to carry me into the woods, I must have registered on the swing of the turn even while I was consciously preoccupied only with light and fresh air.

I had a long walk along that track and I was passing nothing on the way. It was only trees and wild flowers, squirrels, and birds, but it was not my morning for the enjoyment of a nature walk. It was a full half hour before I came out on paved road and there even muscle memory failed me. I had no idea of which might be the better direction to take. I had in mind nothing more than the nearest house where I might beg the use of the telephone.

I couldn't even toss a coin. I searched my pockets for one before I remembered that I had been taken at a time when I had been working on the mess in the apartment and I didn't have a penny on me. I turned right onto the pavement but that only because the word also happens to mean correct. In the absence of any reason, falling back on linguistic mystique had to be good enough. I was hoping for a passing car. If I could get a lift, I was ready to take it whichever way it would be going.

The first car was going the other way. I spotted it coming toward me and immediately turned and raised my thumb. It was a woman, driving alone. I can't say she took no notice of me. At the sight of me, she speeded up and shot past me at lightning speed. She held to that pace for the full time I had her in sight. So that was one frightened lady. Someone less timid would have to be coming along.

Since I was turned around watching her out of sight, I was tempted to try in that direction but decided against it. I told myself that one car didn't have to mean that all the traffic or even most of it would be going in that direction and, going that way, for a good piece of the road I would be retracing my steps over territory where I already knew there was no house. So I plodded on, continuing in the direction I'd been taking before the lady had come along. It was not impossible that I was going to have to walk all the way. I wasn't about to waste any steps.

Then the next car loomed ahead. It was also coming toward me. Stopping and putting the thumb up, I worked at looking harmless. This time the car slowed down and the driver looked me over as he went by. It was a man alone, but if this guy was going to fear anybody, it would have needed to be a behemoth at least one size larger than King Kong. He was not as big as he was chunky, and it looked like a chunk of solid granite. About ten yards beyond me he pulled up and waited, watching me as I ran toward him.

"Sorry, mister," he said. "You can see I'm not going your way."

"It doesn't matter," I said. "Either way."

"It doesn't now? What's your story?"

"I need to get to a phone, a house where I can use the telephone."

"Out of gas? Car broke down?"

"No. I have to call the police."

For what seemed like a very long moment he studied me, saying nothing. I was waiting for him to speak or to make some gesture like leaning across and opening the car door for me. I was being circumspect, not touching the door handle, waiting to be invited.

Moving with great deliberation, he took the key out of the ignition and stowed it carefully in his pocket. Opening the door on his side, he came out to the road and walked around to where I was waiting.

"All right, brother," he said. "Back up a step. Lean forward and lay your hands flat on the hood. Spread your legs."

I came too close to telling him he had been watching too many cop programs on TV. I bit the comment back. I was working on a way I might suggest to him that if he didn't want to give me a lift to the nearest phone, he might call the police for me.

I held it until he had patted me down. Having done a thorough job of it, he enveloped my shoulder in a massive hand and pulled me back to stand upright.

"All right," he said. "Climb aboard. I'll catch hell from the wife for this, but shit. I was a Boy Scout long before I was ever a married man."

I was in the car before he could change his mind.

"Thanks," I said, as he climbed in and got her started.

"It's nothing. We'll be at my place in nothing flat. You understand my being careful before I picked you up. Hitchhiker looks okay. Next thing you know, you're out in the road yourself. You're thumbing because he's robbed you and taken off on your wheels. That's been happening around here too much lately. Just last month it happened to a guy I know, and with him it was a babe done him. They're riding along and she's keeping him real happy with her left hand feeling him up until she comes up with the .22 in her right. He swears he's cured of ever getting horny again, and that could maybe be worse than losing his wallet and his car."

"Crazy," I said. "So mine's crazy, too. I don't even know where I am. I was kidnapped last night out of my apartment. That was back in New York. They held me all night and then they just now dumped me off in the woods."

"That what you're going to tell the cops?"

"That's it generally," I said. "They'll want all the details."

"You can bet your ass they will," he said.

He had been taking us along at a good clip, but now he had moved it up to an excessive speed. He had chosen a peculiar place for it. Houses were beginning to appear at the side of the road, and he was zipping past them.

"Look," I said, "it doesn't have to be your place. Just drop me at this next house. It's only to use the phone."

"It's not going to be my place and it's not going to be anybody else's house," he said. "You just sit still and behave yourself. You're

going where I'm taking you and don't think I'll be holding still for
any shit from you either."

"Now, look," I said.

"You look, mister. You think I'm some kind of dope. I don't know
what your game is. You was kidnapped last night and held till just
now when you was dumped off in the woods? I suppose all the cute
little Disney beasties gathered around and shined your shoes and
creased your pants and washed and ironed your shirt and slicked
you up. Bullshit. I'm not taking you into my house or into anybody
else's house. I'm taking you to the state cops. You can try that
bullshit on them."

"How do I know that's where you're taking me?"

"Because I'm telling you. That's how you know."

I could have tried to explain, to tell him the whole story, to fill
him in on the background. I didn't. I was overcome with the futility
of even attempting it. I could think of nothing in the fuller story
that could in any way contribute to the credibility of what I'd already told the man. More than that, it was obvious that he would
not be listening. I was having the one persistent thought that I had
been through this before. I had been plunged into a world of cham-
eleons where kindly rescuers in a lightning switch converted into
kidnappers.

I had myself so far convinced that it was the pattern as before
that I was waiting for the turnoff into some little-traveled winding
country road. I was eager for that turnoff. I had come to think of it
as my best hope. To wrench my door open and hurl myself from
the car would at the speed he was going be nothing short of suicide. On one of those twisty roads even the wildest driver would
have to slow down. I was seeing it as my only chance.

I had to be ready for it. I tried to sneak my hand toward the door
handle. The guy had his eyes on the road but he had great peripheral vision.

"Forget it," he said. "The door's locked and the lock switch is
over here where I control it and you can't reach it."

I should have known, but even then I didn't want to believe him.
I grabbed the door handle and tried. Of course, he wasn't lying. I
laughed. I'd like to think it wasn't hysteria.

"What's funny?" he asked.

I told him. I was remembering something I'd read years before. A railroad stationmaster, having been told that the company was abandoning his station and that he would be out of a job, was interviewed and was quoted as saying: "Progress gets ahead of everybody."

He laughed with me. "That's for sure," he said.

As he was speaking, he began slowing down and I relaxed. He was as good as his word. He was pulling in at a State Police barracks.

"Thanks," I said. "I must apologize."

"Skip it."

"Before," I said, "I thought I was being rescued, and it turned out I wasn't. I was just being hijacked away from my kidnappers. I got the crazy idea it was happening all over again."

I had been wrong about this guy in a big way, but in a small way I had been right. He wasn't listening. He was giving all his attention to leaning on his horn. It brought a couple of the cops out of the barracks. They came on the run. He took his hand away from the horn.

"I got this here guy for you," he said. "Maybe he's broke loose from a funny factory or maybe he was trying to pull off something. I don't know. Either way he's yours. Take him and let me get along home. My lunch is getting cold and the wife'll be taking the hide off of me in strips. She don't hold with being late for meals."

"What's the charge? What did he do?"

"You're the cops. You find out. How do I know?"

They were getting nowhere. I stepped into it.

"If you will put a call through to Police Headquarters in New York," I said. "Inspector Schmidt, Homicide."

Schmitty's name did it. The cops jumped.

"Mr. Bagby?"

Maybe that won't go down in history with "Dr. Livingstone, I presume," but in my ears it was at least the equivalent.

My astonishment was only slight. I'd expected that the inspector would have been looking for me. It had been hours since he would have first known I was missing. He'd had the locksmith coming around first thing in the morning and he and I had been scheduled to go places. So early on he would have learned that I wasn't in the apartment, and since he would have been confident that I hadn't gone out without calling the precinct, he would have known that there was something seriously wrong.

Actually, however, it hadn't waited till morning. The precinct desk sergeant had been told that I wouldn't be sleeping in the apartment that night and I would be calling him when I was ready to leave. By two o'clock he had begun wondering. Since he knew that I had nothing to sleep on, he'd had no concern about waking me. He rang the apartment. Receiving no response, he had one of the squad cars stop by to check.

The report that came back to him was that the apartment was empty and that the door had been left unlocked. Immediately he'd passed the word on to the inspector. By morning the alarm had been out for hours.

I was in New Jersey, but not as far from Manhattan as I'd thought I would be, only just beyond the suburban rim. Even allowing for the way sense deprivation and anxiety will distort a man's judgment of time and distance, I was certain that I had sped along the Turnpike over stretches that should have produced a far greater separation from the city. I had been adding my ride with my second kidnappers to the one I'd had with my first ones. I had to revise that. The second ride needed to be subtracted from the first. They had carried me in the return direction, part of the way back to Manhattan, though not as far as the Linden cracking plants.

I expected I'd be furnished with quick transport to town. I wasn't. Instead I was given lunch. I was not to be taken to the inspector. He was coming to me.

"What did he do?" I asked. "Put out a three-state alarm on me?"

It hadn't been quite that way. At first light a resident of a back-country area over in Mercer County had called the State Police to report a wrecked car with two men in it, both dead. On checking it out, the cops found the wrecked car pocked with bullets and the two men dead of gunshot wounds. The deaths had not been caused by the wreck. The wreck had been caused by the murder of the two men.

There was no identification on either man and the car bore New York plates. A routine check brought up the license number on a stolen-car list put out by the New York police five months earlier. The information was bucked through to New York.

"New York," they told me, "came right back to us with the alarm on you. They said you had disappeared and they had reason to believe you had been taken from your apartment in a car with that license number."

Schmitty filled that in for me later. When he'd heard from precinct that I was missing, he had immediately questioned the cop who'd brought my message to the desk sergeant. He learned that on leaving me that night the cop had seen a car parked out in the street with two men in it. Suspicious of that, he'd checked the license number and approached the car, only to discover that the two guys were locked in an ardent embrace. He broke up the kiss and moved them on, but he had the number. He had scribbled it in his book. The inspector turned the number up on the stolen-car list.

"A couple of gays wanting to smooch," Schmitty said, "don't do it parked out in the street in a stolen car. Those guys had been there waiting for the officer to leave, and when he spotted them, they came up with this real cute way to fool him."

So the picture had been filling out and then at daybreak the Jersey cops had come through with their big piece. It fitted perfectly. All that would have been needed to fill the last hole in it would have been the discovery of the murdered body of one George Bagby. Inspector Schmidt, therefore, came out to Jersey that day a greatly pleased man. The Jersey State Police had been on a hunt for my body. They had come up instead with a George Bagby who was not only alive and only slightly damaged but also staggeringly well groomed.

He knew who my kidnappers had been. Both of the dead goons had records. They had long been known to the police as a pair of Smiley Donohue's enforcers.

"We can be sure they weren't acting on their own," the inspector told me. "The road where the car and bodies were found is on the way to Smiley's big country place. They were taking you to Smiley. We've picked up Donohue. He was in town and he has the usual fifteen alibi witnesses to swear he was there all night. He's saying the boys weren't working for him anymore. He doesn't know who they were working for and he knows nothing about the stolen car. There's not a thing we can prove on him. His lawyers will have him out even before we're back in town."

Hearing that, I had an inspiration, or I thought I had.

"I kept thinking it was the good-guy-bad-guy routine," I said. "But I was thinking perhaps the lugs hadn't been killed, that the other guys could be lying to me when they said the two were dead, that it might all have been an act. I'm kidnapped. The good guys come along and fake a rescue. I'll be so grateful that I'll give them anything they want. Could that still be it? Would Smiley go so far that he would have a couple of his own guys knocked off just for window-dressing?"

Schmitty shook his head. "No," he said. "That's too far out. Morally I wouldn't put it past him, but he's too smart for it. It wouldn't have been done so close to home, not on a road that leads to his place. Also, he wouldn't sacrifice two of his expert soldiers on something that was hardly a main event."

I had become enamored of the idea and was reluctant to give up on it.

"It could make a great argument for his lawyer to use," I said. "He could cry frame-up."

"Too subtle, Baggy. That's for a storybook. It's not for real."

We took to the road. Leading the inspector and the Jersey cops back to the spot where I had been dropped off in that crazy box was no problem. I retraced the route and walked straight into the place. The box was gone.

"There was a box," I said. "It was right here."

"It was," Inspector Schmidt said, "and they came back and got it out of here. They would do that. They're covering themselves every way. They gave you nobody you can identify and a story no jury can find easy to believe."

"You don't believe it?"

"I'm different," the inspector said. "I know you. I know that if you were making it up, you'd make it a lot easier to believe. Think about your pressed pants, your washed and ironed shirt, your shined shoes. What was all that for? It was to make you look so good nobody will believe you spent the night the way you say you did. The guy that gave you the lift—it's people like him you'd have on a jury."

It was obvious that locating the road into the woods was not going to be good for anything. There were no houses anywhere along it and, as I'd been told, it dead-ended a short distance beyond the spot where I had been left. If there were to be any leads, they could only be in the full statement I would be making. We returned to the State Police barracks for that. The murder of the two goons, after all, belonged to New Jersey as did the second of my two kidnappings.

"The box wouldn't have given us anything," the inspector said on the drive back to the barracks. "The lab boys have been over the letter and the envelope and they're totally clean, not even a smudge to suggest there ever was a print. We need a law against the sale of gloves."

He had more on the letters and envelopes, but as evidence of Homicide Squad thoroughness he needn't have told me about it. I knew his boys were thorough. They had found the machine on which the typing had been done. It had belonged to Lansing Monroe. It had been found on his boat.

"He had this great job," Schmitty said. "Ocean-going stuff. He kept it moored in the Hudson River yacht basin at Seventy-ninth Street."

"That'll be why he was in Riverside Park at night," I said. "He was going to his boat or coming ashore from it."

"You been worrying about what he was doing on the unfashionable West Side?" Schmitty asked.

Back at the barracks I made my statement. It was a long process because I wasn't permitted to scant even the smallest detail. It didn't matter whether it seemed significant to me or not, the inspector and those Jersey cops wanted all of it.

It was obvious that the Jersey lads were something less than ecstatic about what I had to give them. I could be impressed by the care and expert skill that had been exhibited by my second band of abductors, but theirs were crimes that were wholly in the Jersey jurisdiction. In Jersey they had killed two men and in Jersey they had kidnapped me and manhandled me. For the State Police it had to be a disappointment that I couldn't give them any hard evidence on the identities of these people.

What surprised me is that Inspector Schmidt showed delight with my account. He said nothing until I had finished my statement, but I know him well enough to recognize the special glow that creeps up in him only when he has come upon unquestionable pay dirt.

As soon as I detected it, I wanted to go back in my mind over what I had been saying. There had been something there to ignite Schmitty and I couldn't imagine what it might have been. I kept a stern check on myself. I had the remainder of my story to tell. Since I now had the strongest evidence that I had no judgment of what might or might not be useful in it, I was determined to omit not the slightest or most trifling detail. When I had finished, the inspector spoke.

"Good job, kid," he said. "You're a witness in a million."

Grudgingly the Jersey boys added their less fervent thanks. They were wishing I had been witness to something that could have been of evidential value for them. Schmitty spoke to that.

"Not good for much," he said, "I know, but it's all you'll ever get. That's the way it always goes when it's a Jenkins job. You know it's his piece of work, but knowing it doesn't do you any good. You'll pick up Fats, but there's nothing you can prove on him or on any of his people. He's always been slick, but this one looks like his all-time masterpiece."

From the head man of the Jersey crew that drew only scorn.

"That?" he said. "That much we knew right off. Two of Smiley's boys get themselves wiped out, you look at Fats. There's nobody else."

"The way it's been coming at us in our Lansing Monroe killing," Schmitty said, "it's looked like there is someone else. It's had us climbing the walls—a new man in the picture and nobody's even known he's there."

"This hooks in with your Monroe case. It's what Mr. Bagby says. It's what they were questioning him about."

"No question there," Schmitty said. "Fats knows no more about this new man than we do, and it's got him worried. It's got the both of them worried, Fats and Smiley. Look at what they wanted to know from Bagby."

"So what is there in my story that does any good?" I asked.

The inspector explained. Without my account of my night's ordeal there had been no way of pinning it down. I had been kidnapped by Smiley's gang. That much had been established. But these other people—who were they? The Jenkins gang? The new unknown?

"You've cleared that part of it up. It was Fats and his boys."

"I've cleared it up? How?"

"Caleb Sumner. It was Caleb Sumner who took the tapes off you and who gave you the shot that knocked you out for the ride in the box. You didn't see anything of him but a black man's hands and wrists. You can't possibly make any identification anyone could take into court, but it's a positive identification all the same. There just can't be two like him."

The inspector gave me a quick rundown on the man's history. A brilliant kid ambitious to be a doctor had everything it took but the money. He'd gone the route taken by the tough and determined—scholarships, part-time jobs, and loans. It can be done and it is done, but it means starting out under a gargantuan debt burden.

Either because of a financial need greater than most or some mistaken idea that he could hasten matters, Caleb Sumner, in addition to student loans obtained through the customary channels, also went to a loan shark. Since it happened to be a loan business that was a Fats Jenkins enterprise, Fats now had Caleb Sumner, M.D., in his pocket.

"He's paying off," Schmitty said. "But the way the interest at Jenkins' rates kept stacking up, he'd never get paid off as long as he lives. He'd have Fats on his back forever. So Fats is taking it out of him both ways. They've got an arrangement. The way we hear it, Fats is taking cash to reduce the principle. In place of interest Sumner is kept on tap for whatever medical services Fats may need. It's his only way for maybe getting himself in the clear some day—maybe."

"So he fixes up gunshot wounds and doesn't report them?"

"So far as we know, anything and everything," the inspector said. "All the way down to giving Fats a shot in the ass or anaesthetizing Bagby."

I was squirming. "You're not going to ask me to finger him?" I said, hoping against hope.

"I won't because you can't."

I knew his voice. I'd seen his hands and wrists. I could describe the way he worked. All of that added up to nothing that could be taken before a jury. For the inspector it was just another item he could add to the vast store of things he knew and that were of value only insofar as they could clarify his thinking. Their evidential worth was zilch.

The simple fact was that the Jenkins people had handled their job too well. I knew how the man who had given me the lift had reacted to my story. He hadn't believed a word of it. The DA would know better than to waste the taxpayer's money by bringing me before a jury. Nobody was going to believe me. All the great effort to manage so that, apart from the scratches on my face, I would come out of it without a mark on me and to turn me loose impeccably groomed had nothing to do with kindness or humanity. It had been designed for the destruction of my credibility, and it had been a staggering success.

By the time we were through in Jersey and could head back to town it was evening. The program the inspector had laid out for our day was down the drain. Neither of us had slept for thirty-six hours. We were hardly more than started on the road back to town before I corked off. Since the inspector was driving and we did make it back to Manhattan, it can be assumed that he stayed awake. Inspector Schmidt is a man of iron, but once he had pulled up in front of his place, even the iron gave out. We both of us stumbled into the house and fell into bed.

The next morning I woke early but the inspector was up before me.

"Time you got moving," he said. "We're going places."

"Okay," I said. "What places?"

"First stop'll be the gal he didn't marry. Then it'll depend on what we get there. It'll probably be uncle, old man McLeod."

"What about Smiley and Fats?" I asked.

The inspector shrugged. "If you want to," he said, "you can bring kidnapping charges against Smiley and go back to Jersey to lodge the same against Fats. It'll be a waste of time. Smiley swears the two dead goons weren't his anymore. He doesn't know what they were up to and nobody can hold him responsible. We know he's lying, but there's no way of proving it. If we had those two alive, there might have been an outside chance they'd talk, but they're too dead for anything like that."

"What about the way Jenkins and Donohue hook into the Monroe killing?" I asked.

"They don't," the inspector said. "They've just been doing what I've been doing. They've been investigating. We were seeing it as possibly some fresh competition in their territory or maybe as one or the other of them breaking the truce they'd been having. Either way, they'd need to know about that before it could get out of hand. They didn't kill Monroe and they didn't hit your apartment, not either of them."

"If they had no stake in the thing," I said, "they sure have been going to extremes."

"They've got one helluva big stake in keeping their territory and knocking off any third party's attempt to muscle in. Extremes? Kidnapping? A couple of killings? In their line of business that's all in the day's work."

"And the letter?"

"The letter's great. The letter's the thing. It's cracked the case for me. Now it's just cleaning up details."

"I can see that. It shows all over you."

"It does? Good old Dead-pan Schmidt."

"I've been around too long. So how and who? The letter says Fats."

"Maybe you've not been around long enough, kid. You're still not putting two and two together."

"Every time I try," I said, "I get twenty-two."

"You have to believe the letter," Inspector Schmidt said, "and because you believe it, you can't believe what it says."

Such is my faith that I was ready to accept this statement as making sense, but I had not the faintest idea of what sense it could make.

The Griffiths' town house was everything we had been led to expect. It was in the East Sixties and it was the most expensive-looking job on the block. In the East Sixties that is not easily done. It's a big-money district. Inside there wasn't the smallest detail of furniture or decorations that didn't say money. The Griffiths pair received us at their breakfast table.

I had expected that on that morning visit we would be seeing the imprudent Prudence alone, with Eliot out scrambling for the bucks. My first thought was that he was home ill, but after a few minutes I realized that I was disoriented on time. I had lost track of the days of the week. It was Saturday morning. The man, nevertheless, did look ill.

I remembered them from the funeral. She was an exceptionally pretty woman, far too pretty to have gone unremembered. Eliot in his way was, I suppose, even more memorable. When they come that big, you notice them. There had been no lack of muscle that morning in the church. No few of the friends were big huskies and Schmitty's lads, along with the gangland contingents, added up to a lot of sinewy beef. In that company Eliot Griffiths had been a standout. Only Fats Jenkins outweighed and outbulked him, and that was just a mass of blubber. It didn't count.

Now what had been the ruddy flush of good health was gone. The man looked haggard. His face was ashen. He was sunk in depression. It was not impossible that grief over the loss of a good friend might do that to a man, but where had this grief been the day of the funeral? At the services he had looked like a congenitally merry guy who was working hard at holding an expression of suitable sobriety.

"I'm glad you've come, Inspector," he said. "It'll be about that bastard, Lans."

Among friends the word is often used affectionately. Here I could detect no tone of affection.

Prudence remonstrated. "Eliot, please," she said. "What will the inspector think?"

"He doesn't have to think. He's been asking people about the son-of-a-bitch. The inspector knows what he was." He turned back to Schmitty. "I've been thinking I ought to take a walk around to the station house and talk to you people," he said.

It struck me that he had been a long time thinking, but on what we'd been told about him, he could well have been a slow thinker.

"You can talk to me, Mr. Griffiths," Schmitty said.

"Have you got the bastard's gun? I was thinking he may have been killed with his own gun."

"He was machine-gunned. Didn't you see that in the papers?"

"I saw it. It was what got me to thinking it might have been his."

"He had a machine gun?"

"He had one. He kept it on his boat and loaded. Every time I was on the boat I'd unload it for him. I kept telling him it was crazy keeping it around that way loaded, but he wouldn't listen. Next time I'd come aboard there it was again—loaded."

"Did he explain? Did he tell you why?"

"He said it was more fun that way. It made it more like real. I kept threatening him that I'd take it back from him."

"Take it back? Was it yours? Did you sell it to him? Lend it? Give it?"

"I brought it back from Nam. I kept it around awhile, showing it to people. You know the way you do. Then I got so I didn't care about it anymore. It was just kicking around. He wanted it and I didn't. So I let him take it. I been thinking maybe I ought to tell you people."

"And all he ever wanted it for was to have it around for kicks? He never gave you any other reason?"

"No other reason."

"And there was never anything that made you think he might have had a reason?"

"He always went around with a lot of money on him," Prudence said. "I've never known anyone else who would walk around with that much on him."

Eliot dismissed that. "A handgun maybe," he said, "in case somebody tried to mug him, but even that would be stupid. But, hell, a machine gun? You don't go around the city carrying a machine gun."

"Machine gun on the boat," Schmitty said. "Was he running drugs?"

"You know about the cocaine?"

"People have been telling us. Do you know where he was buying it?"

"He'd go up to Canada and bring it down from there."

"On the boat?"

"Geez! You think that's why?"

If the thought had ever occurred to him, he was doing a great job of pretending it had never crossed his mind. Since there was nothing else about his performance that day to make me think he was any good at dissembling, I had to believe the man was that dull witted.

"How about selling it? Do you know where he was selling it?"

"What would he want to be selling it for?"

That seemed a stupid question and the inspector treated it as such.

"Money," he said.

Griffiths laughed, but it was all scorn and no mirth.

"You're talking about Lansing Monroe," he said. "He was made of it."

"It seems like it's always the richest people who feel they can never have enough," the inspector said.

"Not Lans. He was getting the stuff just for himself and to give away. Parties on the boat—he had it there for everybody."

"People have been telling me you were his best friend."

"I was, but all down the line he had me thinking it went both ways."

"But it didn't?"

"Goddamn right it didn't."

"When did you learn that?"

"All the time he had me snowed. So now that's stopped. Dead and buried, he can't snow me anymore. I believed him and I trusted him, but now I know better. I know him for the bastard he was."

All through this his wife was throwing him signals but he seemed to be taking no notice of them. Now she gave up on the signals and spoke out.

"You shouldn't be talking like that," she said. "He's dead. You shouldn't talk like that about the dead."

"Why not? Because I'm talking to the police? I should be pretending I loved him like a brother? The hell with that. I did. I thought we were like brothers. When it happened, I mourned him like a brother. You're afraid people will think I killed him? How's anybody going to think that when I loved the guy? It was only yesterday I got to know he was a liar and a cheat. If I'd had my hands on him yesterday, I'd have broken his neck, but yesterday doesn't count. Yesterday he was already dead and buried. So it wasn't only me he gypped. It was somebody else, too, except that somebody else got wise to him in time. I'm just wishing it could have been me, and I don't give a damn who knows it."

"How did he gyp you, Mr. Griffiths?" the inspector asked.

"If I got wise to him, Inspector, while he was still living, it would be your business. The way it is, it's nobody's business but mine. You don't need to know."

"I'll have to be the judge of that. If there is anything to be known about Lansing Monroe, I need to know it."

"I've told you everything you need to know about Mr. Lansing Monroe. He was a lying, cheating son-of-a-bitch. That's all I can tell about him. Anything else is about me, and you don't need to know about me."

"You can't make that separation," the inspector said. "Your life and his were too closely linked together."

"I know what you're thinking," Griffiths said. "The boy—"

"Begging your wife's pardon." Schmitty gave it his most courtly touch.

Prudence Griffiths giggled. It wasn't embarrassment. It was poorly suppressed mirth.

"We're not Victorians, Inspector," she said.

"And the husband is always the last to know." Griffiths wasn't laughing, but he was not showing any embarrassment either. "Shit! I was the first to know. From the day he was born—no, before that, from the day we were married and actually even before—he's been my boy and never mind whose seed. I'm giving him a brother, and they're going to be both the same to me."

Prudence giggled again while she was giving her belly a pridefully proprietory pat.

"Mr. Griffiths," the inspector said, "you don't seem to understand your position. It isn't good. You had a score to settle with the man, and he was killed with your machine gun."

"You've got my position wrong, Inspector. It's been a long time since it was my gun. It was his. I had given it to him. Also I didn't have any score to settle with him until after he was dead, or anyhow I didn't know until after he was dead. There's nothing wrong with my position."

"Your lawyer is never going to find you a jury that Mrs. Griffiths won't consider Victorian."

"So they'll be shocked. That'll be their problem, not mine."

"Griffiths," Inspector Schmidt said, "I'd like to understand you. You are telling me that you have just discovered that Lansing Monroe betrayed your friendship in some way you consider totally unforgivable."

"Exactly the way it is, Inspector. You understand me perfectly."

"No, I don't. He committed an offense against you that most men would rate as the worst thing he could do to a friend, and you . . ."

Griffiths cut in on him. "Old-fashioned men," he said.

"And undoubtedly lower class."

That was the unflappable Prudence making her contribution.

Schmitty took it with a grin. "Okay," he said, rising to leave. "I'm old-fashioned and I'm lower class, but I've been having a lot of experience with the with-it and the better people, and I have a pretty clear idea of what they have on their minds between the snorts of cocaine. So I'm not without ideas about you, Mr. Griffiths."

Griffiths shrugged. "You must think what you like, Inspector."

"And you don't care to correct my thinking?"

"Not my problem."

"You had better hope it won't be."

"You don't scare me, Inspector. I don't have to tell you anything."

"Quite right, Mr. Griffiths. What you don't say can't be used against you."

Once I realized that Schmitty was going to leave it at that, I couldn't wait to ask him what ideas he did have about Eliot Griffiths. There were, of course, the obvious ideas, but I couldn't get out of my mind what the inspector said about believing the letter but not its contents. I couldn't imagine what that meant, but I could conceive of nothing it could mean that would fit with any ideas one could have about Griffiths.

"Obviously you know what's eating on him," I said as soon as we were out of the house. "I suppose I should know, but I don't. On this one I seem to be missing all the indicators."

"I have all the advantage of you, Baggy."

"We know that. You always have."

"I've seen Lansing Monroe's will. It's something I share with Griffiths and you don't."

I wanted to kick myself. As soon as the inspector said the word, I knew it couldn't have been anything else.

"Not a cent to best buddy and not a cent to the kid? What's he doing, blowing Prudence a kiss from the beyond?"

"Nothing for Griffiths. Nothing for the beautiful bitch. Just a remembrance for the kid and even that has a barb in it. He left the boy the machine gun because it had belonged to his daddy and it was appropriate that Junior should have it."

"You must be kidding."

"Do you think I could dream up a thing like that? Me? Old-fashioned and lower class."

"But what did he think he was doing? Expecting to be murdered and amusing himself by scattering clues to a variety of his potential killers?"

Schmitty shook his head. "You can say these people are unreal and leave it at that," he said, "but that's too easy. He expects he's going to be murdered. You can't think he expects it'll be done with his machine gun and that he just goes on leaving the gun available just so he can play it cute in his will. No, kid, even for these people, that's too unreal."

"Then for this bit there's no connection, just a coincidence?"

"Right."

"Where does his money go?"

"Old man McLeod—'My dear uncle who was more than a father to me.' I guess if you are both with-it and upper class, fatherhood comes unhinged. You can be more than a father or less than a father. Just being a father must have become old-fashioned and lower class."

"Them as has gets," I said.

For part of this talk we had been driving, but it wasn't a long drive. It finished in front of another town house. This one was different from the two we had already visited. It was bigger and it looked older. It didn't look broken down or neglected. It just looked like what it was, a large, old dwelling, solid and sturdy, that had withstood the assaults of time without the benefit of any endeavors to keep it smartened up. The inspector didn't have to tell me that this would be the McLeod house. It looked as though it would be well suited to the old man.

I was busying myself with these thoughts while we stood parked in front of the house. Schmitty was on the car phone. He was ordering a watch placed on the Griffiths' house. It was to be a discreet watch. He wanted the men to keep themselves inconspicuous, but he wanted careful surveillance. I abandoned any line of thought I might have been pursuing when I heard him go into more detailed instructions. Those startled me.

He wasn't interested in either of the Griffiths pair. If either or both left the house, it would be unimportant. There would be no need to put a tail on them. The one he wanted watched was the child. If anyone took the child anywhere, they were to be followed.

"You're there for the kid's safety and nothing else," he said.

I contained myself until he'd hung up, but by then I was sputtering with questions.

"It would be the dumbest, craziest thing the man could do," Schmitty said, "but we have a killer who's been going to every crazy extreme. I can't let myself make the mistake of maybe under-estimating the idiot's desperation."

"Harm the boy as revenge on a dead man?" I said. "That is crazy. But anyhow what's the good of watching outside the house? Griffiths is right there with him in the house."

"Yeah." Schmitty was out of the car. "In the house," he said, "the kid's all right."

Leaving me with those answers that answered nothing, the inspector addressed himself to the doorbell.

CHAPTER 13

My friend Joe McLeod opened the door to us. If on earlier occasions he had looked worn and harried, I wouldn't know how to describe the way the man was looking that morning. He was white-faced. His eyes were bloodshot. He looked as though he had been hit with some devastating illness. He tried to speak and could summon up only a barely audible and totally inarticulate mumble. He wet his lips and tried again.

"Gentlemen," he said, managing a feeble whisper, "could I ask you to go away and come back another time?"

"It's about your cousin," the inspector said. "A few questions."

"I know, but can't they wait?"

"Sorry, Mr. McLeod. They can't wait."

McLeod sighed. He remained planted in the doorway, making no move toward letting us come in.

"My father is sleeping," he said.

"I'll need to talk to the both of you," the inspector said, "but I can begin with you and wait till he wakes."

McLeod still wasn't moving. "We'll need to be very quiet," he said.

Schmitty persisted. "I wouldn't want to interrupt his rest," he said. "We'd like to come in."

"Right now, Inspector, I won't be much good to you. I'm just about dropping with exhaustion. I'm way past making sense."

"Just sitting quietly and talking, it may do you good."

McLeod moaned. "Nothing can do me any good," he said.

He stepped back out of the doorway and we went in. With the

greatest care he eased the door shut behind us. He was guarding against even so small a sound as the clicking of the latch. With a finger on his lips he tiptoed down the hall past the stairs, leading us to the back of the house. There again with the same care he opened a heavy door and ushered us into a large dining room. He didn't speak until he had eased that door shut behind us and even then he spoke only very softly.

"We can talk in here," he said. "His room's upstairs at the front."

"But you won't hear him when he wakes," the inspector said, "or is there someone up there with him?"

"I'll hear him. No fear of that. He has a bell. There's no place I can go to get away from it. Night and day he has me jumping. The dirtiest trick dear cousin Lans ever did me was getting himself killed."

"No replacement for Oliver Williams?" Schmitty asked.

For a moment I was thinking Inspector Schmidt had been holding out on me, but, as they went on with it, I remembered.

"I've had every agency in town sending them over," McLeod said. "Father insists on interviewing them himself. They either come away from that telling me that nobody could ever pay them enough to make them take the old man on or father beats them to it. He takes one look at a guy and orders me to get the bum out of here. He won't have him come anywhere near him. So it's me. Twenty-four-hour duty. Nurse-companion, and I can never do anything right."

"Better than being official avenger of the McLeod family," the inspector said.

"I'm not being let off that one either, Inspector. I've been trying to get that bastard Williams to come back, but he won't even talk to me."

"Williams is awaiting trial on a narcotics charge," Schmitty said. "He was picked up selling cocaine or didn't you know?"

"He's out on bail. He could do it till he comes to trial, couldn't he?"

"He could. Does he say why he won't?"

"Nothing except he was doing it for Lans and he's not going to take it on for anybody else. Lans had him mesmerized or something."

"Something," the inspector said. "They were in business together."

"Business? Lans and Ollie? How?"

"Cocaine. Monroe was bringing it into the country. Williams was doing the selling."

McLeod slapped his hand against his forehead.

"Slow," he said. "Slow, slow, slow. I should have known and I never even thought of it. The minute he heard Lans was dead, Ollie walked out. Never said a word, just up and quit. I thought it was just the crazy way the old man was carrying on. I told myself nobody could be expected to take that. Then, when I heard about his being arrested, I never made the connection, and don't ask me why I didn't. Because Lans was the last person in the world to need it with all the money he had? But I knew him. He was like my father that way. Nothing was ever enough. He always had to be piling it up more and more. Father loved him for that. It made him the true McLeod that I have never been."

"You knew nothing about the cocaine?"

"How would I have known?"

"You were living here in the house. There must have been things you noticed."

"I wasn't here much. I was free back then to enjoy my life. Father was well looked after with Williams here, and Lans was in and out all the time. Father never wanted me around anymore than I wanted to be here. He always preferred Lans. So it was okay. Everybody was happy until Lans had to go get himself killed and make my life a hell."

"His money? From what you say, it didn't all come from his cocaine business."

"Hell, no. I guess that's why I never thought. He'd always had it, even back when we were kids. It was the trust funds then."

Without even asking for it, Inspector Schmidt was handed the full rundown on that side of the Lansing Monroe financial picture, the legal side. There was the McLeod money, a great fortune left in equal shares by the first Josiah McLeod to his only son and only daughter. The son was this Joe's father. The daughter was Lansing Monroe's mother. She died when Lansing was little more than a baby, leaving her estate in trust for him. Shortly after that, Lansing's father, heir to the Monroe money, also died and that was a second huge trust fund for the little boy.

"My father was his guardian and he came to live here. It was then my life began being a hell. Nephew Lansing was automatically better than my father's own son because I could never hope to be more than half as rich as my wonderful cousin. You probably won't be able to understand this, but you don't know my father. Anyone who had all that wealth had to be right in every way. So whatever came up, I was the one at fault. Lansing could do no wrong. My mother was dead, but she'd never had any money of her own. She'd had nothing to leave me. She was his wife, but Father was always contemptuous of her. It was like it was her fault that her father had lost everything in some Wall Street panic before he died, and the blame passed on to me. He had married her with great expectations and he'd been disappointed of them. So what good was she and what good was her son?"

McLeod made no effort to conceal the envy he'd felt of his cousin when Monroe had come of age and came into control of the principal of his two trust funds. He had been out from under old McLeod's thumb, and he hadn't been the one who needed it. That thumb had never rested heavily on him. Then in his majority in control of his money he had handled it like a true McLeod.

"Money makes money and big money makes big money. He spent big, but he was always raking in a lot more than he was putting out and Father thought he was the greatest thing since Croesus and why wasn't I like him? With what? The commissions I could pull in doing my bond-selling job? The only way I was getting by at all was I had the one good customer, Cousin Lans. He did that much for me. He could have done a lot more if he would have gotten his friends to give me their business, but he never did. It amused him to have me dependent on him. Big-hearted Lans."

"Did you know he had a son?" the inspector asked.

McLeod laughed. "I'm not my father, Inspector," he said. "I

knew the dear boy was no angel. He had no wings, but he did have balls. You're thinking of the Griffiths kid. I've heard the gossip."

"Has your father heard it?"

"I've never mentioned it to him. I've known better. He would have had it that Lans was the best friend I could ever have and I was a stinking louse for trying to run him down. I learned that when I was still a kid. Not at Daddy's knee but across it. When I was punished for things Lans had done, if I said it wasn't me but Lans, all it ever got me was a worse licking. I soon learned. With Lans it was like with the dead. Of him you said nothing but the good."

"People have been talking."

"They haven't been talking to Father. He doesn't know those people and he would never listen to them."

Schmitty looked at his watch. "He's been sleeping a long time," he said.

"Not so long."

"The old may sleep a lot, but it's all in short snatches. They sleep and wake, sleep and wake. What time did he fall asleep?"

"Just before you rang the bell."

"For an old man even that's been a long time."

"That's calm old men. They do that dozing and waking all the time, but not my father. When he wakes, he starts raging and he excites himself too much to doze. He doesn't go off again until he's totally exhausted, and then he sleeps longer than other old people do. You saw him at the funeral. All through the service and the drive to the cemetery he never dropped off even for a moment."

"I'm going to have to see him."

"Inspector, you must do me a favor. Don't ask me to wake him. Every minute of peace I can have I need. I'm falling apart. Look. Just go away. Tell me where I can reach you. I'll call you and tell you when you can come and talk to him. Actually it's as much for your benefit as it'd be a lifesaver for me. If I can tell him you're coming and ask him to give you an appointment, then he'll feel all right about it and you'll be able to get along with him. That's the way he'll want it—that you have come at his pleasure. Any other way he'll be outraged and you'll have nothing from him but his telling you in twenty different ways that you are an intruder and that he will have the Mayor deal with you."

"I'll have to take that risk," Schmitty said.

"Inspector, please. I'm begging you. I'm at the end of my rope. You can't imagine what it's like. I can't get anyone to stay with him, and now even the servants have quit."

"The servants? Did your cousin have them running dope too?"

"No. I don't think that, but I'm past the place where I know what to think. As far as I can make out, there was the pay they were getting, but my father didn't know that Lans was doubling it. So there it is. I just haven't got it. I'm not Lans. When I hit the old man to give them a raise, he wouldn't hear of it. He refuses to believe that it's less than the going rate. He just tells me that's what's wrong with me: I don't know the value of money. Then I made the mistake of telling him that Lans had been doubling it."

"I'm sorry," the inspector said. "I must see him. It can't wait."

"He makes a hell for me of his every waking moment. It's bad enough if he wakes on his own. If I wake him . . ."

He let it go at that, indicating that he had no words to describe it.

The inspector was obdurate. "I'll wake him," he said. "I'll take the rap."

McLeod shook his head. "It'll make no difference," he said. "It'll fall on me. I'm in charge. I would have allowed you to do it. Lans would never have permitted anyone to disturb him."

"Maybe he won't want to talk to me," Schmitty said, "but I have Bagby here with me. He does want to talk to Bagby. The other night, after the funeral, he was trying to reach him at his club."

I could read that as only the wildest stab in the dark. There had been those calls for me with the caller hanging up before they could get me to the phone. Those could have been from any nuisance. Actually, however, they hadn't been. It looked as though Schmitty had hit it.

"I know that," McLeod said. "All evening he couldn't make up his mind. He'd call and then he'd change his mind and hang up. Then he'd change again and it would be the same all over again. Finally he did make up his mind. He sent me to talk to George.

Surely George told you about that. I was to talk to George and Father talked to the Mayor."

"George told me and I also heard from the Mayor. His room? Upstairs and at the front, you said."

McLeod jumped to the dining-room door.

"You're not going up there."

"I'm going up and you're coming with me to show me the way."

"Inspector, I'm begging you. You can rouse him up and walk away from it. I'll be here. I have to live with it."

"I have my job to do," Schmitty said.

"You don't do it here. I should never have let you in the house. Now I'm telling you to go. You have no right here."

"But I have, Mr. McLeod. I have a warrant."

"A warrant? A warrant for what?"

"For your arrest, Mr. McLeod."

"Me? What for?"

"For the murder of Monroe Lansing."

McLeod laughed. "You had me scared for a moment, Inspector. That's a very bad joke."

"No joke. You tried too hard. You ended up outsmarting yourself. Faking the burglary in Bagby's place was a lousy idea, and then you didn't even do it well. You should at least have taken the silver and made it look like a real burglary, but you took nothing. You were there to plant that stupid forged letter and you didn't even do that well. You put it in a place where it never could be hidden. With the letter shoved under the lining the book couldn't be forced back into the case. It was obvious all along that the letter hadn't been there and overlooked by the burglar. It had been put there during the phony burglary."

"What letter? I don't know what you're talking about."

"But you do, Mr. McLeod. You made a further mistake. You wanted to make sure that the letter would be found and quickly. So you placed the book and the case right out on top of all the other wreckage you caused. You left it sitting on top of the stuffing you'd pulled out of the sofa upholstery. That made no sense. Somebody looking for a letter, ripping everything apart in a search for it, might go so far as to look for it to be sewn inside upholstery, but it would be the last place he'd look. He would have gone through books and papers first. If he had looked through the books and missed it, the case couldn't possibly have been on top of the upholstery stuffing. It would have been buried under it."

"So what? What has any of that to do with me?"

"On top of all that you were still pressing. When you went around to see Bagby the next day, it wasn't on your old man's errand. You came on your own to make sure the letter would be found. You found it for Bagby."

McLeod sneered. "On a pipe dream like that you come here and accuse me of murder? Not a word of it is true, and even if it was true, you couldn't prove any of it. The one person in the world who is really hurt by Lans's murder is me. I never had any reason to kill him and every reason to want him alive. He was all I had to keep the old man off my back. With Lans gone I haven't a hope. I'm under the old man's heel and no way out. Whatever little freedom I could enjoy is wiped out. You know Lans was dealing in drugs, and you don't do that without getting mixed up with the gangs, and the way he was killed—everybody knows that's the way the gangs do it. You know all that and you ignore it to build this crazy thing on me. Okay. Try and prove it."

"Exactly what I am doing," the inspector said. "The next step is to talk to your father. He'll tell me whether you were with him the night of the burglary. He'll tell me whether he was trying to reach Bagby that night or if it was you checking on whether you'd have the apartment available for your game."

McLeod opened the dining-room door and held it open for us to go through.

"Very well," he said. "He'll tell you and I'll tell him what you're up to. Then he'll put a call through to the Mayor and I'll see you out of the house. May I tell you, Inspector Schmidt, that it's you—you're the one who's outsmarted himself."

I could hardly believe that the inspector could be out on a limb and about to be chopped off, but I was shaken. McLeod's sudden about-face had me baffled. All his dread of the hell he would catch for waking the savage old tyrant had been replaced with eagerness for the forthcoming confrontation between the inspector and the old man.

To expect that he could have had the old man primed to lie for him about where he had been the evening of my pseudoburglary or about the phone calls to the club was beyond my imagining. I could only think that he knew his father and that he was expecting that the murder charge against his son would rouse in the old man all that McLeod blood that was thicker than water and that it would be McLeods against the world and young Joe securely safe behind the McLeod wealth, the McLeod political clout, and the McLeod attorneys.

He led the way up the stairs and to a closed door at the front of the house. There he paused with his hand on the knob.

With an air of the greatest consideration he addressed the inspector. "You're sure you want to go on with this, Inspector," he said. "It's your neck and your career. Perhaps you'd like to change your mind or at least have a little time to think about it."

"I'll worry about my neck," Schmitty said. "You worry about yours."

McLeod turned the knob and pushed the door open.

"All right," he said. "Your choice. Go on in and wake him up."

"You first," Schmitty said. "I want you where I can see you."

McLeod shrugged. "As you like," he said.

We were no more than in the door when the inspector grabbed McLeod's arm and dragged him across to the bed. It wasn't that McLeod had been hanging back. It was rather that suddenly the inspector was moving fast, and even in this hurry he was serious about keeping the man where he could see him.

At the bed he bent over the old man. I joined them there. Old McLeod was lying on his back. His eyes were open and he was still. It was that stillness that can never be mistaken for anything but what it is—death. The inspector put his hand to the body.

"Cold," he said.

"Dead? He was sleeping."

"That's not sleep and it hasn't been for some time. The Medical Examiner may be able to give us a line on how long."

McLeod gulped. "You mean a *post mortem?*"

"Yes."

"I won't allow it. You can't without my permission."

"You're wrong about that. He went without a doctor in attendance. It's required."

"No, it isn't. He was under a doctor's care. The doctor will sign the death certificate. His heart. It's been expected."

"He's off your back."

"That's a lousy thing to say, Inspector."

"Mr. McLeod," Schmitty said, "you are under arrest for the murder of Lansing Monroe." He turned to me and indicated a bedside telephone. Asking me to call it in for him while he read McLeod his rights, he turned back to his prisoner. I made the call quickly. McLeod waited until I had hung up.

"George," he said, "your friend hasn't decent respect for anything. Since he is not even permitting me to close my father's eyes, could I ask you to do it for me?"

I started to turn toward the bed. The inspector stopped me.

"No," he said. "Nobody touches him."

McLeod protested. "Inspector. This is inhuman. It's barbaric."

"It's necessary. A feeble old man has been alone in a house with a man charged with murder. At the old man's age and in his condition death may be expected at any time. It also might be hastened by a pillow pressed over his face."

"He was my father."

"We may not be able to prove this one even after we've had the Medical Examiner's findings and we've seen the will, but it doesn't matter. One murder is enough."

When all the evidence was in, there was good reason to believe that it had indeed been two murders. On what Inspector Schmidt had for him, however, the DA felt he could make a better case on the Lansing Monroe killing. So Joe McLeod was tried and convicted on that one. The DA would have preferred it the other way since, if convicted of his father's murder, McLeod could not have inherited under his father's will; but, handling it as he did, the DA had a sure thing and he couldn't risk sacrificing that.

There was evidence that the old man had been killed, but it was too thin to offer a jury. The contents of the dead man's stomach placed the time of his death as almost immediately after he had eaten his breakfast. With no servants in the house the breakfast had been ordered sent in from a local coffee shop. The coffee shop people had a record of the time of delivery at the McLeod house. The timing didn't fit with McLeod's statement that his father had been alive only moments before we had arrived at the house.

When questioned about that he said that between the time he'd ordered the breakfast and the time it had been delivered, his father had fallen back to sleep. He had waited till the old man had wakened again and had reheated the breakfast. The DA had no confidence in his ability to persuade a jury not to believe reheated fried eggs.

The old man's will was a beaut. He left everything in trust for his son with the trust to be administered by his nephew, Lansing Monroe McLeod, with the principal to pass into the control of Josiah McLeod, Jr., only on the death of Lansing Monroe McLeod. Income from the trust adequate for his maintenance was to be paid to Josiah McLeod, Jr., in sums determined by Lansing Monroe McLeod. This provision had been made since Josiah McLeod, Jr., had demonstrated no competence in the handling of money, and it was to be hoped that his cousin in the course of his lifetime might be able to teach him what his father could not.

I wondered aloud how Junior could have known about the will.

"In that family he was a cinch to know," Schmitty said. "He'd have had it both ways. Dear cousin would have told him for the fun of seeing him squirm, and Daddy would have been sure to tell him as part of the process of rubbing in on him how much better a McLeod dear cousin was than he ever could be."

"And he had been looking forward to the old man dying and his being a free man at last only to discover that he would just be switched from papa to cousin and no reason why that wouldn't be for the rest of his life."

"Plus Monroe taking the McLeod name," Schmitty said. "What little freedom he'd been having he'd had only through Monroe. He'd been glad to have Monroe keeping the old boy happy. Between that and the business Monroe was throwing his way he had been having some kind of a life. Then suddenly he sees it the way it is. Monroe has been sucking up to the old man and cutting him out. He was probably afraid that if it went on, there would be another will with everything going outright to Monroe."

"That would never have happened. He's a McLeod and their blood *is* thicker than water."

"Sure, but the name change must have shaken him."

"The car chase after he was in my place? The shots? What was that?"

"Either the Jenkins crowd or Smiley's. They were worried and sniffing around. Whichever it was must have been outside your place watching, and they thought your burglar would tip them to what was going on. So they chased him. He managed to lose them. There was a repeat of it on the kidnapping. The Smiley gang snatched you. The Jenkins mob was watching, followed, and grabbed you from them. They had to know what was going on. They had no more than that to do with it."

"But how did McLeod know they'd show at the funeral?"

"He didn't. He just planned for his killing to look like a gang job. Their turning up at the funeral was a break he hadn't expected. It fitted perfectly with what he'd planned to do. He'd already written the letter. He couldn't have gotten to the typewriter after the funeral. We were on the boat by then. When he was feeding you that bull, he said he recognized Smiley from newspaper pictures but he didn't know who the fat guy was. Jenkins has had his picture in the papers at least as much as Smiley, but he'd fingered Fats in the letter, so in talking to you Fats would be the one he didn't know."

"You knew from the first it was no burglary, even before the letter."

"He'd overdone it. There was too much wreckage. Just making that much mess would have filled the evening. There wouldn't have been the time for looking through even a small fraction of the stuff we were supposed to think had been searched. It was phony at first glance. The only question was who. Then he helps you find the letter, and that tells me who. The rest is just clearing away the camouflage and pinning it down."

"One other thing," I said. "It's really nothing, but I can't figure it. All those flowers. Where did McLeod get the money for that?"

"Monroe went around with too much cash on him. Monroe's corpse paid for its own flowers."

This was only the smaller indication that Daddy McLeod had been right in his estimation that when it came to money his son was not a true McLeod. There was an odd situation that had the DA squirming. McLeod was convicted of the Monroe murder and therefore should not have been permitted to benefit financially from his victim's death. However, since the inheritance of Monroe's money had come to him not under Monroe's will but as contained in his father's estate, and he had not been found guilty of his father's death, the money did come to him.

Prudence Griffiths sued on behalf of her baby son, claiming the Lansing Monroe estate on the basis of promises made to the boy. No one for one moment imagined that in our Victorian courts her suit would have a chance, but Joe McLeod settled with the lady, giving her half of the part of his inheritance that had come from his cousin's estate.

No true McLeod would have parted with it.

ABOUT THE AUTHOR

GEORGE BAGBY is the pen name of an author who has been honored with the Grand Master Award, the Mystery Writers of America's highest distinction. He has been writing crime novels since 1935. He was born in Manhattan and has always lived there, when not on world travels. The most recent adventures of Bagby and Inspector Schmidt of the New York Police Department are THE GOLDEN CREEP, THE SITTING DUCK, A QUESTION OF QUARRY, and COUNTRY AND FATAL.